Tangled Roots

Marianne K. Martin

Bywater
BOOKS

Ann Arbor
2014

Bywater Books

Copyright © 2014 Marianne K. Martin

Bywater Books First Edition: October 2014

Printed in the United States of America
on acid-free paper.

Cover designer: Bonnie Liss (Phoenix Graphics)

Bywater Books
PO Box 3671
Ann Arbor MI 48106-3671
www.bywaterbooks.com

ISBN: 978-1-61294-053-3

For Jo

Who has always known

"The most important kind of freedom is to be what you really are. You trade in your reality for a role. You trade in your sense for an act. You give up your ability to feel, and in exchange, put on a mask. There can't be any large-scale revolution, on an individual level. It's got to happen inside first."

Jim Morrison
(in conversation with Lizzie James)

PART I
Atlanta, Georgia 1906

1

There was a clear parting of the ways as children made each other aware of Grandma Addy's approach. Anna and Nessie, however, were too engrossed in their make-believe puppet world and reveling in the laughter of their captive audience to notice.

But when the laughter stopped abruptly and all eyes shifted to above her head, Anna knew. Her puppet's arms fell limp and Anna turned to find her grandmother staring down at her.

"You need to be tending to your guests."

"Maybe they would like the show, Grandma. It's so much cooler here and we could make some benches—"

"No, they are waiting on you to open your gifts. You mustn't keep them waiting." Addy turned her head to leave, then turned back. "I'll have a couple of the older boys bring the theater over to the tent."

"Yes, ma'am." There was a hint of winning the compromise in Anna's expression. "Come on, Nessie. We'll do the show all over again for them."

Nessie stood but made no attempt to follow Anna.

After a few steps alongside her grandmother, Anna turned to see that Nessie was still standing behind the theater. "We'll get the puppets after I open the gifts, Nessie. Come on."

Nessie stood silently, her eyes now focused on the ground.

"Nessie will stay here, Anna, while you entertain your guests."

"No," Anna replied, marching back toward Nessie. "They're not my friends, they're Emily's. And, they're boring."

Grandma Addy's eyes held their stare. "I'll have no back-sass from you. You will mind your manners and entertain your sister's friends, too. They came here to celebrate with you."

3

"But, it's my birthday," Anna replied, staying her ground and taking Nessie's hand. "Why can't I have my best friend there?"

Nessie stood silent and lowered her eyes.

Grandma Addy stepped toward the girls, her words softening to a story-telling tone. "It must be, that's all. When you're grown some, you'll see. You'll both see." She held out her hand to Anna. "Come on, now."

That was it. There were no legs capable of holding a stand against Grandma Addy. Anna leaned over and whispered something to Nessie, and held her hand until Nessie nodded, then Anna took her grandmother's hand.

Halfway to the back of the house, Anna asked, "What won't I know 'til I've grown some?"

"What's proper, honey child. That's all. Just what's proper."

It was supposed to be a wonderful day. A birthday celebration better than all others because she had the perfect gift for Anna, the absolute perfect gift. And, for Nessie, the day had started out to be just as perfect as her gift.

"Hurry, hurry, hurry. Lest you make your momma worry." The words had bounced breathlessly with each long stride of ten-year-old legs. Nessie hurried along the well-worn path to the big house on the hill. It was going to be the best surprise ever.

Despite her wide-brimmed hat shielding the rays of an intense September sun, perspiration ran dark streaks down the smooth brown skin of Nessie's cheeks.

"Hurry, hurry, hurry," she chanted again, excitement quickening her steps as she neared the house and the voices busy in preparation.

A burlap bag of tomatoes, fresh from the garden, fought the skirt of her blue cotton dress, and the cloth bag slung over her shoulder safely carried Anna's birthday surprise. Such a party; days of preparation. More than any birthday that she could remember. It had taken days for the boys and men, straight from the fields, to erect the huge white tent, haul out tables and benches, and tend the fire until the coals were

4

white-hot perfect. Nessie loved the sounds, the voices, the anticipation. But it was the smells leading to a celebration that she loved most. The sweet smell of pork roasting on the spit filled the air, wafting through open windows to challenge the aromas of rising yeast and warm fruit pies. After all the anticipation, the day was finally here. Nessie's smile gleamed wide and bright as she ran the last few yards to the back door of the big house.

Inside the kitchen, large flat pans of cornbread cooled on a long table and pans of bran muffins were being pulled from the oven. The huge blades of the overhead fan pushed hot air in a futile attempt to temper the heat.

Nessie ducked under her mother's arm and reached for a muffin from the basket on the counter.

"You bring the best tomatoes, child?"

Her mouth already full of a large bite of sugar-crusted edge, Nessie nodded and raised the burlap bag up off the floor.

Willa Jameson peered inside, looked over the first few fruits for quality, and handed the bag to Nessie's aunt at the sink. "Uh, huh, you did pick good ones," she said, with a kiss to Nessie's head. "Now, take this rag and get it cold under the pump and bring it back for Grandma Beulah's neck. Hurry on, now."

Nessie rushed out the back door, anxious not just for her grandmother's comfort, but to quicken the time to when she could give Anna her present. The old pump stood chest high, a few yards from the back door, and from there she could see the corner of the big tent on the east side of the house. Nessie watched as she pumped the handle. More than the usual birthday guests were spilling beyond the poles. She didn't recognize any of them, all white women, dressed in their Sunday best, or the girls hanging close to their skirts.

The water turned ice cold and Nessie doused the rag under the flow and rung it out. She gave one more curious glance toward the tent, then hurried back to the kitchen.

"Oh, thank you, thank you, child," her grandmother said, closing her eyes and smiling as Nessie wrapped the cold rag around her neck. "This here cake's gonna get iced now free of ole Beulah's sweat drops." Her laugh, with that soft lilt at its end, made Nessie smile. She could always pick out her grandmother's laugh from the mingle of voices and laughter emanating from the kitchen at night, and it helped put her to sleep.

"Go along now," her mother said, filling another basket with warm muffins. "Put Miss Anna's present on the bench in the hall. And take this basket to the table under the tree."

"But I wanna give Anna her present."

"You do that after her guests leave," she said, turning Nessie's shoulders toward the hall.

It wasn't right. It wasn't right at all. Nessie slipped the cotton bag from her shoulders and left it on the old oak bench that had lion's paws at the end of the arms. Her brothers and her cousins and the other farm workers' kids were all gathered under the big tree on the west side of the house. Pine boards stretched over sawhorses served as tables for the tin plates and cups and enough food to keep them all happy. This is where they usually gathered, everyone, Anna's family, too—celebrating birthdays, adults sharing stories of the week while children laughed and played. Under the tree on the cool side of the house. The tent, usually reserved for weddings and holidays, had Nessie wondering.

Two muffins were snatched from the basket before Nessie could put it on the table with the breads and pies. Henry, her cousin, running from John Allen and too fast to make the turn, caught his sleeve on the corner of the board and nearly upended half the table. He was grabbed by the nape of the neck by the closest man and their tag game redirected to the open yard.

"Papa," Nessie called, as the tall, lean figure emerged from around the huge trunk of the tree.

"Got it all set up right back here," he said. "Went together just right."

She followed him to the other side of the tree where a huge root, protruding and running atop the ground, made a perfect seat for four small butts. "Look here how nice it is," his tone brimming with pride at his handiwork.

"Oh, Papa," Nessie exclaimed as she examined the puppet theater with its new wooden floor and fresh black and gold paint. "It looks like real, just like in town." The wooden structure, while sturdy and perfect for two little bodies working hand puppets from below, had remained unpainted and devoid of decoration since her grandfather had made it years before. It had taken only one trip to town, though, to the Grande Theater where cousin Little John worked, for Nessie to fall in awe.

The sight had stopped her short just inside the big doors—grand indeed, with its fluted columns on either side of the stage and scrolls of gold across the top. The normal stream of questions that Nessie would have asked, bombarding Little John, never had a chance to form. She stood there speechless, her eyes moving slowly over details and color and a grandeur that she had never seen before.

"Come on," he said, "ain't nobody here this early." He took her by the hand and ran down the center aisle, around to the steps, and onto the stage. There they were, blood red curtains framing their presence, standing where the talents of actors and singers and dancers shone in the spotlights.

Little John threw his long arms out to the sides, lifted his face upward, and turned a slow, full circle. "Up here," he said, "you can be anything and anyone."

Nessie saw the joy on his face, threw out her arms, twirled around, and claimed that joy for herself.

"You could be Ma Rainey and sing the blues and dance, and everyone will applaud. And I," he added, easing lazily into shuffle-tap steps on the balls of his feet, "can be Mr. Bill 'Bojangles' Robinson."

Nessie smiled and tried to mimic Little John's fancy steps. "Who would Miss Anna be?" she asked.

"Well," he said, repeating the steps more slowly so that Nessie could copy them. "Miss Anna don't need to be up here on this here stage to be whatever she wants."

When Nessie got home that day, she and Anna made their hand puppets sing like Ma Rainey, and that's when the plan for the most perfect birthday present ever was set in Nessie's mind.

"Look here," her father said as he bent down to pull little blood red curtains across the front of the puppet stage. "Your grandma sewed 'em up special. And, see here? You can paint a different piece

7

of paper and put it up in the back, so's you can be outside, or in the kitchen, or any place ya want."

"It's so pretty, Papa. Let's hurry and show it to Anna."

He straightened his long frame and spread his hand gently over Nessie's head. "Time 'nuff later for that. You let Miss Anna tend to her guests. Go see if your momma needs you."

It seemed downright silly to get all dressed up in your Sunday finest to celebrate a birthday. Anna scowled her way down the stairs. Her beige cotton dress with the big pockets was just fine. It made no sense to have to change. And why in the world did Emily have to invite *her* friends? It wasn't *her* birthday.

Grandma Addy greeted her at the end of the hall. "Anna, honey, take this up to your momma's room." She handed her a plate with a warm, buttered, blueberry muffin and a glass of lemonade. "She's not feeling well today. This is her favorite, so it might pick up her spirits."

It wasn't that Anna minded. She didn't at all. It seemed as though it wasn't her birthday party anyway, with Emily's friends from school and church there and the adults making all the plans. It was just that she hated to see her mother on her "bad" days. She had known it would be a bad day for her mother the moment she got up this morning. The sound in the house was always different on those days. Quiet. Not a church quiet, like when the preacher is giving his sermon. It was a sad quiet. A hush, wishing not, but knowing better.

Anna walked carefully along the squeaky boards of the upstairs hallway, but couldn't say why. She placed the glass on the floor, and rapped lightly on her mother's bedroom door. When there was no response, she picked up the glass and entered cautiously.

"Momma?" She spoke softly as she approached the bed. "I have a surprise for you."

The room smelled of not caring, like Jane Buffet at school whose hair and clothes rarely got washed, and Daniel Jenkins's breath, and being all shut up together with no air to push it away. It did no good to hold her breath; that only made her take a big gulp of nasty air at the end.

She placed the plate and glass on the bedside table and tried again. "Momma, it's my birthday today."

Her mother's eyes were open, her head turned on the pillow to stare at the closed drapes on the opposite side of the room. But she didn't stir.

"Grandma sent you a muffin and lemonade, and there's lots of good things to eat. And Nessie's grandma made my cake. You have to come down so that I can blow out the candles."

A tiny spark lit inside Anna's chest when her mother turned slowly to face her. That same tiny spark which tortured her over and over by dying so quickly. "No," her mother replied as if it was painful to speak. "You go on. Leave me be now."

"But you promised that you would play the piano. Everyone loves it when you play and we can sing . . ." Anna reached out and smoothed down the dark auburn hair over her mother's forehead. "I'll brush your hair 'til it shines and pin it up for you, and I'll get you the pretty dress with the lace on the collar . . ."

But the spark that had held the tiniest of hope was gone. Her mother turned her face away and there was nothing left to do.

So far, today had been special only in bad ways. Papa had business in town, Momma wasn't feeling well, and Emily got to invite her boring friends. Well, *Emily* can play the silly, stupid games with her friends. Anna hurried down the stairs, stopping at the bottom for just a glance toward the kitchen, then headed for the front door.

From the porch Anna could hear the clank of horseshoes and squeals of laughter from Emily's guests on the lawn. Anna ran down the steps, past the Beautyberry bush and was almost knocked over by John Allen racing around the corner. Losing his balance, he tumbled to the ground and was quickly tagged by one of the Jackson twins. "I'm sorry, Miss Anna," he said, rubbing his elbow as he jumped to his feet.

"Hey, John, you're 'it'," she said and laughed. "Where's Nessie?"

"The other side of the tree. They're gonna have a show in the theater."

"Oh, yes," she replied, breaking into a skip, "we'll do a show."

She jumped over the big roots of the old tree, felt the immediate

9

coolness beneath its massive branches, and welcomed the sight of Nessie's smile.

"Oh, Nessie, look at the theater. It's beautiful." She examined it closely, stooping to open and close the red curtains. "What a great surprise."

"There's more, there's more. That's only part. I'll be right back."

Nessie ran as fast as she could, in the back door and through the kitchen, and grabbed the cotton bag from the hall bench. Somehow, amid the bustle of kitchen activity, she slipped unnoticed back through the kitchen with her prize.

"What is it, Nessie? What is it? I can't wait to see," Anna exclaimed as Nessie breathlessly presented the bag.

"We made it for you, Papa, Grandma Jameson, and me," she said with a smile so big it showed all her teeth.

In an instant, Anna pulled from the bag a string puppet. A beautiful string puppet—face and hands of smoothly carved wood, silky brown hair, and a pretty hand-sewn yellow dress.

"Do you like it?"

"Yes, yes, I love it," Anna said, quickly wrapping her arms and the puppet around Nessie's shoulders. "It's the best birthday present ever," she said, squeezing her tightly.

Then, with a quick release, she added, "Come on, let's do a show."

It took only minutes for the strings to be unwrapped and tested, and hand puppets to be retrieved from below the theater floor. "What shall we name her, Nessie? Who will she be?"

Nessie's eyes widened with possibility. "She can be *anyone*."

"Emily." Grandma Addy's tone was one wrong look short of major irritation. "I told you to find your sister. Is she still up in your mother's room? She needs to just leave her be when she's having a spell."

"No," Emily replied. "She's under the tree, putting on a puppet show with Nessie. I told her she needed to be playing the games under the tent, but she said they were boring and it's cooler under the tree."

Before the last few words had left Emily's lips, Grandma Addy, jaw set determinedly, was hard-stepping her way to the other side of the house.

That's when the perfect day ended.

That's when Nessie knew that the rules had changed.

2

It was a long way back through the overgrown field abandoned when the reduced workforce could no longer farm it. Sitting in the farthest corner, also abandoned, was a tool shed just waiting its new lease.

Nessie could see the slant of the old tin roof, but couldn't tell yet if the door was open or closed. Although she had run a good distance of the way home from school, she had no doubt that old Jona would have had Anna home in the buggy easily before her.

Concentrating on her school lessons had been near impossible all day. From the moment she had gotten there, until the moment she bolted from the door of the converted old church building, Nessie had thought of nothing but meeting Anna at the tool shed. It had only been a whisper, quick and direct, no details at all. But one thing was clear, Anna had a plan and it was meant for no one else. It was going to be a secret.

She tried to hurry, but the tall grasses grabbed at her skirt and tough stalks twisted her black leather shoes that were a good size too big for her feet.

Finally, she could see the door standing ajar and a piece of board tossed from behind it, then another. She hesitated to call out until she saw the light brown head of hair with its telltale braid falling over Anna's shoulder. "I came as fast as I could," she called as she closed the distance to the small clearing.

Anna reappeared from behind the door, her face red from exertion and bright with whatever secret she was about to share. "Nessie, this is perfect. Come and see." She pushed the door open wider and Nessie stepped around a pile of boards to follow Anna inside.

Anna stood in the middle of the little building, her biggest smile directed right at Nessie. "Isn't it perfect?" she asked, taking both Nessie's hands. "This will be our place. And no one's going to know, and when we're here no one's going to tell us what to do."

Nessie looked around, beyond the spider webs and the piles of boards and broken-handled tools—and she saw it, too. A good clearing out and sweeping, some discarded pieces of furniture, and yes, it would be theirs.

"Come, on," Anna said, her eyes darting from wall to wall, "help me take all this stuff and put it in the old wagon around back."

They worked tirelessly, clearing everything they saw no use for, and using sticks to wind up cobwebs and discard them outside. The sweat covering their arms and faces had traded its glisten for a layer of dust and dirt. Nessie pulled up the hem of her skirt to clean her face, and Anna burst into laughter.

"What?" Nessie asked. "Didn't I get it all?"

"It's your hair," Anna replied, with a pat to the top of Nessie's head. "You look like an old woman." She started trying to pick loose the dusty grey net of cobwebs clinging to the wiry nap of hair that was tied into little tufts.

"What?" Nessie asked. "What is it?"

"Cobwebs. And I can't get them off."

"You have to, Anna. Momma will want to know where I've been."

"And, that just wouldn't be proper," she replied in her best Grandma Addy imitation. "Being out there in that dirty ole tool shed."

"My momma wouldn't say that . . . but, Papa told me about why your grandma was so mad at the birthday party. You got to worry about your 'proper' friends now."

Anna pushed Nessie's head down a little so that she could reach the tufts at the crown of her head. "I looked it up in the big dictionary at school today. I thought there might be a special meaning. But, it just means suitable, like I thought. And, just because Emily thinks they're suitable, doesn't mean that they're suitable to be my friends."

"Papa said that knowin' what's proper is the most important thing to know."

"All I know is that they're boring. They're like Emily; all they

13

talk about is boys. All the time. They tell secrets about seeing a boy's privates and all. Stupid. Not good scary secrets like we have."

Anna picked the last of the webs from Nessie's hair. "There," she said, "you're proper again."

"Did you see the Billy doll in the guest room when you went upstairs to see your momma?"

Anna shook her head. "I was going to look when I got her dress out, but she didn't feel well enough to get dressed."

"Do you think it's up there?"

"Grandma Addy said that she put it up high so that we couldn't mess with it. The armoire in the guest room is the only place left that I haven't looked."

"Why doesn't your grandma want us to play with it?"

"Must be a grown-up secret."

"About why the hat keeps falling off?" Nessie lowered her voice almost to a whisper. "Do you think there's a ghost?"

"We're going to find out, just you wait."

"I guess you couldn't go tellin' your proper friends about the ghost. That's just for you and me."

Anna held her hands up, palms out, and Nessie did the same. They grasped right hand to right hand, and said together, "You and me." Then left to left, "Best friends we." They pulled their hands and locked their arms tightly, "Locked together, secrets forever."

Saturday afternoon was the best time to see if they could find the doll, with Anna's momma feeling good enough, and she and Emily going to town with Anna's papa. As soon as Nessie's papa had his lunch and headed back to the barn to fix the mule harness, her momma told her to "get along and play" after the kitchen was cleared, so Nessie met Anna under the big tree.

"Do you think Grandma Addy is sleepin' yet?"

"She went right to her nap after she finished puttin' up the beans for tomorrow," Anna replied. "Come on."

They ran around the front of the house to the corner where

Grandma Addy's window was partially open. Carefully the girls stepped around drooping red blooms in desperate need of water. Anna held her finger to her lips and the girls listened below the window. Yes, there it was. Interrupting the surrounding hum of fan-pushed air was the deep, intermittent rumble of Grandma Addy's snore.

Nessie failed to stifle a high soft giggle. Without tempting fate further, the girls ran around to the back door, and carefully closed the screen door behind them. At the foot of the stairs, Anna warned in a whisper, "Remember, step exactly where I step so you don't hit the squeaks."

They reached the top without one misstep, and walked along the outside of the carpet runner to avoid the squeaky boards. Once in the guest room, Anna went right to the armoire across the room from the foot of the bed. She tried the doors, but they were locked.

"This *must* be where Billy is," Nessie whispered, "because it's locked up. Grandma Addy sure don't want us to play with it."

"Maybe I can find the key," Anna said, beginning a search of a small wooden box on the top of the bureau. They found no key, and moved on to the drawer in the table next to the bed. Nessie watched. Still no key.

"I'm going to look in Momma's room."

Nessie followed Anna across the hall, and watched from the doorway. The search covered the jewelry box, the drawers, and even the sewing basket. But, there was still no key.

Disappointment clear, Anna said, "Grandma must have it." She crossed the hall again to close the guest room door, grasped the door-knob, and froze. "Ho," she gasped.

"What?" Nessie asked, crowding closer to a clearly frightened Anna.

"Look," Anna whispered.

Nessie looked into the room where Anna pointed. There on the floor at the end of the bed was a small replica of a Union army cap. The cap that matched the war uniform which they knew the Billy doll wore.

Nessie wasted not a second. She bolted down the hall and clambered down the stairs, with Anna so close on her heels that she almost pushed them both down the last few steps. Sounds, half-stifled screams, escaped them both as they raced out the back door and around to the far side of the big tree. They grabbed and held each other tightly and huddled at the base of the trunk.

"The ghost," Nessie whispered, barely catching her breath. "I told you."

Anna tightened her arms around Nessie and nodded against her head.

Then came the sound that snatched their fear, and nullified it in an instant. "Anna Elizabeth," Grandma Addy shouted, "you come up here on this porch this minute. Do you hear me?"

The girls separated with a start. "Yes, ma'am," Anna called back. "I'm coming."

They appeared appropriately demure at the porch steps. Grandma Addy stood in the doorway, arms folded across her chest, her expression diffused behind the screen door. Her tone, however, was quite clear.

"I cannot think of one good reason for you girls to be making that kind of ruckus in this house."

They waited, eyes dutifully trained on the figure behind the screen door. There are times when silence is the best defense. They chose it wisely.

"Is there a good reason?"

They answered in unison. "No, ma'am."

"Then you best find something quiet to do until everyone gets back from town. You hear?"

"Yes, ma'am," was offered quickly. And, just as quickly, they accepted their reprieve and hurried out of sight.

Neither of them said a word. They ran to the edge of the field, and made their way as fast as possible through waist-high growth to the shed, their own little "house" now.

Nessie closed the door behind them, collapsed onto the stool with the broken rung, and barely caught her breath. "Oh, Anna, she's really mad at us."

Anna nodded and settled on the discarded kitchen chair. She started to wipe her face on the sleeve of her blouse, but Nessie stopped her. "No, use your skirt. Remember?"

Anna was never able to make her clothes last as long as Emily's before they needed washing, but Nessie's trick helped. Anna pulled her skirt up and wiped her face with the underside of the hem.

Sunlight, from an old window with a crack the width of one pane, streaked across Anna's flushed cheeks. "I'll brush Grandma's hair out for her tonight. She likes it when I do that."

"You gonna tell her 'bout Billy's hat?" Nessie asked.

Anna shook her head. "She'd be even madder knowing why we woke her up . . . you saw it, didn't you? Right there on the floor."

Nessie nodded. "I saw it, just like you. What's that ghost want with Billy's hat?"

"Papa says there's no such thing as a ghost, but if there was it'd be knocking that hat off because it's just not right that that doll's dressed in Union blue. He says it's got no business being in this house since Grandpa was a captain and died for the cause and all. He even said that to Grandma Addy."

Nessie's eyes widened. "What'd she say?"

"She straightened up tall, and pushed her shoulders back like this, and said, 'This is my house. What I choose to keep here is no one else's business, and you will do well to remember that, Mr. Benson.'" Anna relaxed her posture. "She never calls him Thomas when she's that mad, it's always Mr. Benson."

"It's best not to get your grandma mad, that's for sure."

17

3

Thomas Benson was particularly fond of the new sign displayed prominently above the glass door. Satin black, it spanned the width of the entrance and announced with fancy gold letters in a graceful arch: T. K. Benson Insurance. It was fitting of a prominent Atlanta business. He needed only to be able to take the next step and land a prominent, wealthy client for his company to be seen as a serious competitor to Thacker & Son. And Benson Insurance would have gained the respect as a leader in the business community in half the time that it had taken Old Man Thacker.

He stood at the edge of the walk, hands on his hips, and surveyed his sign, looking at it just as he imagined potential new clients did. It was by far the best looking sign on the street, and it surprised him that he had yet to hear a compliment from another business owner in the two weeks it had been up. Thomas went back up to the door, locked it, and checked its security, then took one more long look at the sign before starting down the street. Today, he'd take the time to have lunch at the club, mingle with the fraternity of business owners, and collect a few compliments there.

An hour later, though, there had been cordial greetings and ongoing discussions of weather and stocks and the gubernatorial race— and not one compliment about his new sign. In fact, as Thomas moved about the smoke-filled room lined with bookshelves and game tables and dotted with groupings of chairs perfect for conversation, he hadn't found one opportunity to mention it.

He dared not interrupt Ben Johnson, stern in his concentration to avoid checkmate, or disturb the intensity of a poker game with a pot larger than his last three months' earnings. No, today he'd have to settle for the bar, a good cigar, and a few small business owners like himself.

He ordered a beer and joined George Wagner, who owned the tobacco shop, and his brother at their table.

"I've got to say, George, this is a fine cigar you recommended." Thomas drew his lips around it, turned it slowly, and drew a puff as he tilted his head back.

"A little more expensive than some," George replied, "but you can't argue with that flavor, and every puff is cool on your mouth. Yes sir, a good smoke, good friends, and a good woman, and you got life by its tail."

"You'd better throw a good job in there," Gerald added. "Not much of a good life to be had without it. Damn Negro businesses are taking over, taking money right out of our pockets."

"It goes without sayin', little brother, we make Clark Howell our next governor so he can put 'em back in their place."

Thomas nodded. "He's got my vote. If we don't get control of this now, there's no tellin' what's next. Too many of 'em already think that voting will make them the same as us. There's an article in the *Journal* every day about another white woman being accosted. I got my wife and my girls to worry about."

"We all have to be takin' care of our women." George took a long sip of his beer, then leaned over the table to focus only on Thomas. "How *is* your Mary?" He asked. "Genevieve said that she saw you all in town last Saturday."

Thomas held off on the next puff, and leaned forward in his chair. "Sickly more days than not," he said. "Got Doc Jones baffled and searchin' his journals for some answers . . . It's worrisome, George, worrisome for me and the girls."

"Well now, you let me know if there's anything you need. Genevieve can have our girl cook you up some supper, or take your daughters for a spell after school. It would be no bother, no bother at all."

"That's a kind offer, George. Much appreciated, but we'll manage. Business is doing well now. I'm thinkin' I'll hire some more help for Mary. You know, someone—"

A hand on his shoulder brought Thomas's attention to the club's security guard leaning close to his ear. "It's your foreman, Mr. Benson. You need to hurry, sir, there's been an accident on the farm."

Thomas rose quickly, excused himself and met John Shakly, his hat clutched tightly in both hands, standing just inside the door.

"It's Miss Mary," he blurted. "Take my horse, it's faster. I'll bring the buggy. Hurry."

Thomas rode the miles to the farm with the vigor of his youth, carrying a fear too heavy for even a lifetime of strength. *An accident.* Hooves pounded the dirt. Thomas gave heel to the horse's sides. *What kind of accident? Has she fallen?* The horse stretched forward. Powerful strides. Loud snorts and heavy breaths. *What could be so serious, so urgent? What has she done?* A long ride, so much longer now that it was weighted with worry. Thomas pressed the horse harder.

The horse was tiring, slowing his stride, but the house was finally in sight and Thomas urged him on. The dust at the top of the drive was still settling. Doc Jones's carriage was visible, parked at the rear of the house.

Thomas dismounted quickly, nearly stumbling as the horse took its last few steps. He bolted through the back door, saw no one, and rushed to the bottom of the staircase. He called Mary's name, his voice jetting anxiously, and received no response. He called her name again, then his mother-in-law, Adeline's. Then he rushed back outside. "Mary, where are you? Doctor?" he called, hurrying toward the open door at the side of the barn.

Doc Jones met him in the doorway, placed his hands on Thomas's arms to keep him from entering.

"What is it, Doc? What's happened?"

"I'm sorry, Thomas," he replied. "She's gone. There was nothing I could do."

"Mary? No, no, not my Mary." His eyes pleaded for better, pleaded for hope. "She's not gone. That can't be, it just can't be."

He tried to push by, but the doctor held his ground. "Adeline is with her now. Give her a little longer. Come with me so we can talk." He urged Thomas gently toward the back steps. "There's nothing more to be done."

Dazed and compliant, Thomas sat on the top step, with the doctor settling next to him. "I know this is hard to hear, Thomas, but you must know." He waited for Thomas's eyes, wide, anxious. "It looks as though Mary shot herself. And, with the depression . . ." The doctor placed his hand over Thomas's shoulder. "No one needs to know that it was anything but an accident. Just an accident," he said, squeezing Thomas's shoulder, "that's all."

Thomas leaned forward and buried his face in his hands. The day seemed to taunt him—bright, cloudless oblivion to his unfolding gloom. He rocked forward and back, fingertips digging into his hairline. Then he lifted his head and stared straight ahead. "But, it wasn't, was it, Doc?"

"She had pain, Thomas, the kind we can't see a cause for, one we couldn't take away with medicine. She only wanted free of it . . . she just didn't know another way."

"What am I gonna do?"

"Right now, you mourn your Mary," he replied, rising from the step. "And, comfort Adeline. She'll be talking with the girls when they get home from school."

Thomas rose and followed the doctor to the barn. He would see his Mary, steel himself to what had happened, to the loss, to the implications. He would be the strong one, the one to keep this family together, and hold the others up. He vowed it, willed it, as he walked through the door.

But his knees barely held his weight at the sight of his wife's lifeless body. Adeline knelt in the dirt and straw next to Mary, alternately smoothing auburn-brown hair back in place and wiping off her own tears as they splashed onto her daughter's forehead.

No words came, no utterance of grief or consolation. Nothing. He stood, unable to move, unable to will his shaky knees to the ground.

The doctor knelt next to Adeline, placed his hand on her forearm, and spoke softly. "She's at peace now, Addy. No more pain. Let her be now. We'll take care of her. Come on," he said, his arm around her, his hand under her elbow. "We'll take good care." He helped her to her feet. "The girls will be home soon. They're going to need you."

Thomas watched them leave, watched Addy straighten herself,

standing to her full height a few inches taller than the doctor. He still had no words, nothing of use, only muted half-thoughts struggling for reason.

Thomas stole a look at his Mary, paler than she was fair, but could not avoid seeing the ugly wound to her chest. He lost control of his legs and crumpled to the dirt next to his wife's body. "Why, Mary?" he managed. His hand shook as he reached to touch her shoulder. He pushed it gently as if to wake her, as if it would prove wrong what he saw, what he heard. When it didn't, when he touched the cool flesh of her cheek, he forced himself to his feet.

His legs quivered still as he walked to the door of the tack room. He rubbed his forehead without purpose. "Why? You had everything you needed." He slammed his palm against the door. "How could you do this?" He turned, dropped onto the nearest bale of hay, and buried his face in his hands. "How could you do this?"

Something about the day made Nessie run to their place faster than usual, sooner than usual. They had no special plans for today, no new book to share until tomorrow. No news yet from cousin Little John about when he could get them in to hear the new singer at the theater. Nothing to warrant the urgency.

As much as she had hurried, though, not stopping to talk with anyone after school was dismissed and not walking partway home with Jenna to hear all about her latest crush, Nessie should not have beaten Anna to their place. Yet, their signal board, held by a rusty nail on the corner of the building, remained untouched.

Nessie pulled the broken end of the board free with her fingertips and raised it to signal Anna that she was there. Their place was just as they left it each day; it always was, because no one knew about it yet. Emily was busy with her friends after school, often late to do her chores and counting on her grandmother's forgiveness. The boys, Nessie's brothers and cousins, were counted on to feed and water the livestock and clean the barns. When they finished, they would rush off to swim in the creek or imagine they could pitch like Cy Young or hit like Nap Lajoie. None of them were inclined to bother about what Anna and Nessie did with their time. Nessie could read their thoughts as easily as she read a book—girls' stuff was boring, and only Daniel, Uncle Joshua's boy, was old enough to realize why anyone would waste a perfect baseball afternoon sitting in the back of a wagon with a girl.

So the secret place was safe and all theirs. Nessie pulled a folded piece of white cotton fabric from her bag and opened it onto the small table that Anna had rescued from the scrap pile. It would have been burned for firewood otherwise, and it was the perfect size for their little house. She smoothed the material over the top—so much prettier than the old scratched surface. Her surprise for Anna today. She could hardly wait to show her. It's proper now, she'd say, and then offer her best smile.

But, what could be keeping her today? Tomorrow was rug day, and they would beat them together to make short work of it. Their plan was a good one; they did the same chores on the same day so that they would have time together. Tonight they would each mend socks after dinner, so now should be their time together.

Nessie poked her head just far enough outside the door to look across the field toward the big house. Nothing. No Anna running through the tall grasses to meet her. And nothing visible past the corner of the barn.

She ducked back inside as a horrible thought sent her stomach muscles into a tight spasm. What if their secret had been found out? What if Emily had sneaked and followed Anna one day, just to see, and told her momma or Grandma Addy, or even worse, told her papa? It would be the end, surely. No more time with Anna. No time to share and laugh, and dream about what could be. He would put a stop to it all, even quicker than Anna's momma would. That was sure.

Only Grandma Addy seemed to let it be, to turn her head to the friendship still there. If only it were up to her, the last word hers, and hers alone. Wouldn't she find Nessie to be a proper enough friend? Wouldn't Grandma Addy find her worthy? Anna could tell her how they studied Anna's books together, books a full year ahead of Miss Tilton's school lessons. And how fast she learned the lessons and how she knew the answers to the quiz questions sometimes before Anna did.

But none of that would matter if Anna's papa knew they were still best friends. She'd heard him say it, that day just as they were beating the last of the rugs. "... the Robins girls, and George Wagner's daughter. I told your momma to arrange for you to spend time with them. Someday you'll understand, it's important to make the right friends."

Maybe that's where Anna was now, at her new friend's house. Maybe her momma did arrange for it, now, right during their special time together. Of course it would be now, directly after school and before chores. She would ride home with them and stay until Anna's papa picked her up.

The possibility, the realness of it, churned the acids in Nessie's stomach. She lunged toward the door, sure that her lunch was on its way up. She hung her head out the open door, felt the muscles of her abdomen tighten and spasm. Again, and twice more. But nothing came up. Nessie clung to the latch on the door, bent over and unable to stop the quivering. She couldn't bear even the thought of it. To not have Anna's friendship, to not see her everyday. No, she would not be able to bear it.

Again she looked to the field. Still there was nothing. No Anna, skirt held up high and honey-brown braid bouncing, running along the path to meet her. Momma had warned of this day, tried to prepare her. But, it had always been a far-off day, a maybe never day. Yet, even as her mother had spoken the words, they had taken on a distance, been carried away on a puff of air. So, how could it have come so quickly? How could it be so real, so fast? A plan past that day, past this day, had never been allowed to form. *Don't think it and it can never be. And now, what to do? What to do?*

The quivering traveled to her legs. She couldn't stay here any longer, couldn't allow it to be real anymore. Nessie dashed from the little building, forced her legs into a shaky run, and pushed her way through the field toward home. *Keep going. Faster, faster. Just get home. Everything will be okay, everything will be fine. Just get home.*

She burst into the house, and banged her elbow hard against the doorframe as she rounded the corner into the kitchen. Breathless and unable to stop the sobs, she threw her arms around her mother's waist and buried her face in the faded flowered apron.

"Oh, child," her mother said as she held Nessie tightly to her. "Dear child. There, there." She pressed her lips to the top of Nessie's head, held her there for a moment. "Shhh, shhh." She kissed her head again. "Did Jackson tell you? I told them boys not to say, to let me tell you when you got home."

Nessie tried not to hear the words. She pressed her face harder to her mother's breast, breathed deep the familiarity, and held it. *No, don't say, don't say.* The arms around her would take the hurt away, surely they would.

"Come on, now. Come along to Miss Addy's and help me fix a chicken casserole for their dinner. It'll make you feel better. Your grandma is busy helping Miss Addy prepare Anna's momma for the viewing."

It took a moment for the information to tear its way through the fearful tangle of emotion. That's what it had been, just her own fears, woven tight and hardened into a truth that wasn't there. *Not there at all.* But in its place was a truth nearly as hard to face.

She lifted her face, wet with spent tears. "What happened to Anna's momma?"

"There was an accident," she replied, wiping the palm of her hand over her daughter's cheeks.

It was real: Anna's momma was dead. *And what about Anna?*

"Oh, Momma," Nessie finally managed. "Momma." *How could you stand to lose your momma? How could Anna?* "Can I see Anna?"

Her mother nodded. "I 'spec poor Miss Anna's gonna need her best friend 'bout now. But when we go in you wait 'til I say, you hear? A family needs to grieve together."

It didn't feel right. Nessie waited in the kitchen while her mother checked on Anna's family. There were long moments of silence, the natural hum of daily life halted, changed. She waited, wishing back the sounds of sisterly fights and teasing laughter, the hustling of chores, the familiar. Instead, only interludes of low hushed voices and soft crying interrupted the silence. She stood obediently near the doorway, hands in her apron pocket, shifting from foot to foot. Then came a sound that split the silence and raised goose bumps on Nessie's bare arms.

Emily, she was sure it was Emily, wailing. No words, only a tear-wrenching wail that caused Nessie to cover her ears with her hands and move to the far end of the kitchen. Emily eventually quieted, but Nessie stayed behind the end of the table until her mother returned with Anna.

"Nessie, you girls go outside for a spell 'til I need some help with dinner."

They settled on the bottom step, shoulder to shoulder, neither of them speaking until Nessie asked, "Did you see your momma?"

Anna nodded, staring at the toe of her shoe as it pushed a semi-circle in the red soil. "Nessie," she began softly, "I think I heard a secret." She turned and looked into Nessie's waiting eyes. "I wasn't supposed to hear."

"What was it?"

Anna took Nessie's hands. "You can't tell."

"You know I won't—ever."

Anna nodded. "Dr. Jones was talkin' to Papa and sayin' that no one must know. Momma hurt herself with a gun. He said that she didn't want to be here anymore."

"Why do you think, Anna? Why did she get so sad?"

"It was me and Emily always fussin' and fighting. I just know it was. Oh, Nessie, why did I fight with her so?"

"Emily is always startin' you to fightin'."

"And, the flower beds," Anna continued, "I promised and promised to weed 'em. I didn't know it would make her so sad, Nessie. I truly didn't. And, now it's too late. It's too late." Anna's chin was trembling and her cheeks wet with tears.

"You can tell her you're sorry. Pastor Emmons says only the body dies, and we all got a spirit that keeps on livin'. My grandpa talks to his papa lots o' times, and he died long 'fore I was born. He says his papa helps him figure out things and not get mad when things don't go right." She could see that Anna's chin had stopped quivering, so Nessie pressed on. "And Pastor Emmons says that all the bad that happened to our body, like if our heart gets to hurtin' or our back gets all bent over and painful, that the spirit is free and don't feel none of that after."

Anna released Nessie's hands, and wiped the tears from her cheeks. "What about Momma's sadness?"

"Your momma's spirit gave up all that sadness. There ain't no way she can be sad now, 'cause she'll see the prettiest sunsets ever, and all the flowers are beautiful and got no brown edges, and the music and the singing is sweeter than sugarcane. Only ones sad now are the ones missin' seein' her, 'cause you got to wait so long to see her again."

"Do you really think I'll see her again?"

"As sure as that ole sun gonna come up in the morning."

Time had ticked by without Addy's notice. She hadn't moved from the straight back chair next to Mary for hours. The room had grown dark except for the low-light flicker of the oil lamp. She couldn't leave her even now, even when there was no more chance to hear her voice or to tell her how much she loved her. And she couldn't accept good-bye, not yet.

She made no attempt to stop the tears, only blinked clear her blurry eyes to focus on Mary, to take in the last of her while she could. So little time left to see her face, her beautiful fine features, the porcelain-like skin. Her baby. Peaceful, as if she were merely resting after a long day—furrows gone, no worry-drawn lines. *Is that consolation enough, should it be? To know that the pain is gone, the pain that there seemed to be no answer for? There should be relief, gratefulness that Mary is free of it now.* Instead, the questions blared through Addy's thoughts, desperate for reason, for understanding.

Why hadn't there been an answer, a way to help Mary through the unexplained sadness. *Was it the babies, the sadness driving Thomas away? I tried, Mary, caring for the babies. But, they wanted you, needed you. What did I not see? What was it that no one saw? Whatever it was, I would have faced for you. There is nothing I wouldn't have done, if only I had known what it was. Nothing could have been harder to for me to bear than watching the glint of joy leave your eyes, to watch your daily struggle for happiness. I would have done anything to bring back the playful smile that I loved so much, or the sound of your laugh, sweeter to my ear than the finest symphony.*

Addy placed her hand, warm and gentle, over the cold thin hands folded below the lace bodice of Mary's favorite dress, and whispered, "You had so much goodness in your life, your music, your girls, a husband and a home." She caressed the cool smooth skin of Mary's cheek. "Why wasn't it enough? What was so heavy that it took it all away?" *I always thought the strength would come, that there would be a day when you pushed aside the sadness, when you saw it had no power over you.*

The doubts began where the questions left off. They were unrelenting, pressing Addy for reason or at least recognition of her complicity. It was her responsibility, after all, to give her child the means to deal with life's disappointments, to handle its injustices, to find happiness. And she had clearly failed. There was something that she had not given Mary, something intangible. Addy had tried to pass on the blessings that her own father had given her, to teach the same lessons to Mary. She encouraged her to ask questions, and experiment with solutions, to put the pieces together herself and test the whole. She had challenged and respected her young daughter's mind, just as Addy's father had done. Yet Mary had tired of it early and given up easily. Only music had held her interest, giving her focus and bolstering her confidence. A gift and a talent that still, in the end, had not been enough.

Missing from Mary was the strength and determination that had allowed Addy to take on the challenges of the difficult times. Raising a child without a father, running a farm without a husband, she'd heard the talk and fought the expectations. Horrible to have lost a husband, a father, but you must find another; God intended it, people expected it. A woman's constitution, they said, is not capable of the responsibility, her mind and body will only break down from the stress. But she had proven them wrong, hadn't she?

Still the question remained unanswered. How is it that one can summon the needed strength and another cannot? *I don't understand. What did you need?*

Maybe a necessary anger—the same sometimes barely harnessed fuel that drove Addy past the odds. Or the indignation that spurred her each time she was dismissed or disrespected. *Maybe Mary never felt that.*

Addy closed her eyes—just for a moment, she promised, just long enough to pull back visions of the happy times. She needed to see the young inquisitive eyes looking up at her, holding such promise, to see her smile again so bright and pretty. Mary smiled so easily then, laughed and danced with such happiness.

Yes, I can still hear it, your beautiful laugh, Mary. Such a beautiful sound. I need to hear it. I need to always be able to hear it.

Addy squeezed her eyes tighter, the tears came anyway. She blinked them clear again. Too little time left to be with her baby. Too little time before saying goodbye would surely take the air from her lungs.

4

"Be *strong* in the Lord," Pastor Cecil Price's voice boomed over the large congregation of the Methodist Episcopal Church. "Reach out to Him," he continued, "and let the *power of* His Spirit *lift* you from the depths of your despair."

Anna lifted one knee and then the other, trying to unstick the back of her legs from her sweat-soaked dress and the hard, oak pew.

Grandma Addy laid her closest hand on Anna's arm and fanned herself faster with the large paper fan decorated with white magnolia blossoms. It was her silent message to stop fidgeting and fan harder. But it didn't matter how fast Anna moved the cardboard paddle, it only pushed stale, hot air against her face. And to make matters even worse, it invited larger whiffs of sickeningly sweet perfume from the woman with the wide, white linen hat sitting in front of her. The choice was clear: it was better to sweat more and gag less.

Emily didn't fidget, at least not noticeably. She fanned, dainty and quick. Hardly worth the effort. Like an undersized adult, she sat straight and proper, and listened—or at least pretended to, and rarely gave Papa cause to remind her of sermon etiquette.

Anna snuck a side-glance to confirm her sister's trancelike state, eyes closed, fan barely moving. How she managed it for such a long time was beyond Anna. It didn't seem possible to ignore the incessant rise and fall of the pastor's voice, pounding home a message about sin and redemption that Anna didn't understand.

All she could think of was how she wanted Nessie to tell her more about what Pastor Emmons said. About the beautiful place where her momma was now, the pretty sunsets and the sweet music. She needed to know if her momma's spirit could see her, and see how hard she was trying not to argue with Emily. Maybe he knew if Momma could hear her when she said how sorry she was, and if Momma was smiling when she got all the weeds out of the flower garden. Nessie said that he knew all about those things—and that's all Anna wanted to hear right now.

"Yes, a horrible accident, just a *horrible* accident." Thomas said it over and over, untiringly, as sympathetic church members offered their condolences.

"Whatever will you do, dear man?" the woman with the awful perfume said as she clutched Thomas's hand. "You poor, poor dear. My daughter Millie and I were talking just yesterday about what a tragedy it is for such a devoted man as yourself to lose his wife so young. Our sincerest prayers go with you."

And so it went, for long after formal church time had ended. Addy and the girls had moved at a much quicker pace, accepting sympathies and briefly answering well-intended questions. They waited at the buggy while Thomas continued shaking each hand, leaning intimately toward their words, their sentiments, extending every minute to its fullest. There were people Anna had never seen exchanging more than a cordial greeting with her parents before, but he continued nodding and talking as if they had shared evenings together in the parlor.

The early afternoon sun was beginning to erase the more comfortable morning breeze and Anna tugged at the lace-trimmed collar standing stiffly around her neck. She unbuttoned the top two buttons and stretched it free.

"We're not home," Emily said, her tone bearing a close resemblance to a motherly reprimand. "Button yourself up. Papa will be embarrassed."

"It's too hot," Anna replied. "Papa needs to hurry up, and you . . ." Anna stopped—not because Grandma Addy was turning around, or because Emily had the right to her bossiness, but because she had made the promise. If her momma was finally feeling good, it would not be Anna who took the smile from her face anymore. "You never mind," she said quietly to Emily, and then re-buttoned her collar.

31

Thomas walked slowly, still listening intently to Pastor Price. As they reached the buggy and Thomas shook his hand, the Pastor addressed Addy.

"Your family will remain on our prayer list, Miss Adeline. My wife and the ladies will be calling on you this week."

"It is appreciated, Pastor," she replied with a nod.

The isolation from his family became more apparent than ever after they returned home from church. While Addy set the girls to writing thank you notes for the many kindnesses they had received, Thomas retreated to his library alone.

Moments later, Addy tapped on the library door. "Thomas, I need to speak with you."

"Yes, yes, Adeline," he muttered forlornly.

She entered the room and approached the large, brown, leather chair where Thomas was already nursing his first bourbon and branch water.

"What is it, Adeline?"

"We need to talk about the girls," she replied. They had had only one discussion like this between them up until now. It had been necessary, but uncomfortably outside the parameters of what Addy considered her role. Her talks with Mary had been different. Talks between a mother and daughter are tethered: an arterial tether that flows and feeds, sometimes freely, sometimes not. But its existence is undeniable. There was nothing that affected one of them that did not affect the other. Joy flowed one to the other, like air lifting light and fresh. And the pain, toxic, unstoppable, was made bearable only by the girls. Until five days ago.

"They will need you to attend to them, Thomas, now more than ever."

He made no attempt to look at Addy. Instead, he stared ahead at mahogany bookcases with glass fronts and the Captain's old secretary desk—his chosen domain, dark noble lines, stately marks fitting of a respected businessman. He held his glass loosely with fingertips and thumb, relaxed his wrist, and rested his elbow on the arm of the chair.

A practiced gesture, a distinction that far-removed him from the crudeness of his sharecropper father.

"A man has to have time to grieve," he said before taking another swallow of bourbon.

"We all need to grieve in our own way." Addy stepped around the matching chair on the opposite side of the lamp table. "But, they are only children. They need their father."

"They have their father. You can't expect more than that. A man can't be both mother and father to his children."

Addy took a moment to carefully select her words. There wasn't a lot she truly liked about Thomas Benson, aside from the fact that he seemed to love her daughter and had remained faithful to her. Years ago she had tried talking with him, only to realize that no amount of asking would result in him giving Mary what she had really needed from him. The special alone time that Mary so desperately wanted from him had disappeared soon after Anna was born. And despite Addy caring for the babies in order to allow Mary to be with her husband, there were countless reasons that interfered with their time together.

There used to be three reasons to be patient with him, now there were two. "Anna is sure that it was things that she did that caused her mother to leave her," Addy began. "And, Emily is terrified that something may happen to you, too."

"I can't explain to Anna what caused this tragedy," he replied. "I don't understand it myself." He finally turned to make eye contact with Addy. "I'll have a talk with Emily."

"It's not so much your words they need, Thomas. They need your time, your attention. Emily is learning to play the piano; she would love for you to listen. And, Anna loves books and playing card games. Maybe you could spend some time in the evenings with her."

"Yes," he said with a nod, "of course." He turned back to his bourbon, savored another swallow. "Much of what they looked to their mother for, though, they will have to get from you now."

The truth was that much of what they should have been getting from their mother, Addy had been providing for a long time. What she held now was only a small bit of hope that Thomas would expand

33

his view of fatherhood to fill at least a little of what the girls needed. Time would have to judge that hope.

"They will always have the best care I can give them. Have no doubt of that," she said. "Shall I send them in before they go to bed?"

"Yes, I'll do what I can to reassure them."

5

Reassurance rode safely atop their father's words, until the promises turned to empty air. It hadn't taken long, just past a month. For the girls, that time hadn't been measured in days or weeks, but in smiles and nods and promises kept. And, when the measure fell short, the effects were clear.

Addy occupied her usual end of the love seat, darning the last sock as music from the phonograph played in the background.

Anna rolled the last of her already darned socks and placed it in the basket. "Done, Grandma," she said, jumping up from the footstool. "Can I go now?"

"Be back in time for dinner, and—"

"Papa's not coming. Why do you make me wait for nothing?"

Why indeed? Maybe it was cruel on her part, to hold a hope that Anna had already recognized as lost. But, unfulfilled needs tore at her being for reasons far beyond today. Addy looked into Anna's eyes. Such a sadness there, childhood sparkle dulled. Anna would do much as she herself had done, shove the need aside until something took its place. Imperfect to be sure, but there was strength there—so much like her own, and enough to get her through.

"Nessie's momma is making her favorite cornbread, and she said that she would be delighted to have me come to dinner with them. That is, if it is all right with you. And after dinner we'll put on a new puppet show for the little kids."

Anna flashed a smile at Addy's nod, and turned quickly to leave.

"Wait, child," Addy said, reaching for her hand.

Anna turned back, her smile dissolving as she took her grandmother's hand.

"Sometimes it's hard," Addy began, enclosing Anna's hand in the soft sureness of her own, "identifying love, knowing what it looks like. It's best to close your eyes and just feel it. That way you can remember the times when you felt loved—when your momma smoothed the hair from your forehead and kissed your sweet cheek, when your daddy picked you up and twirled you around 'til you lost your breath and hugged you while you laughed. And now, every night when I tuck you safely in your bed and sing until you sleep, you'll remember what love feels like. It's the most important thing, Anna. It's the best anyone can give you."

Anna wrapped her arms around her grandmother's shoulders and hugged her tightly for a long moment. "I love you, Grandma."

"Yes," Addy replied softly, "and I love you—more than sweet potato pie and a long rain on dry crops."

Anna released her and stood. Her smile had returned.

"Always remember to close your eyes," Addy said. "Now off you go."

6

Finding her mother's journal hadn't been the purpose of Emily's search, only a result. There had been no real purpose: it had just begun one day after school. She stopped in front of her mother's bedroom and moments later she was lying on the bed, pressing her face into the cotton pillowcase, and trying to breathe in some tactile remembrance.

Lying on the bed that day had led to another, and then visiting her mother's room had become Emily's daily routine. The visits soon included sneaking looks into dresser drawers, timid touches of her mother's belongings, and now regular readings from two small journals written in her mother's hand.

Emily quietly closed the bedroom door, retrieved the second journal from its place under her mother's scarves in the top drawer, and sat on the floor behind the bed to read.

THURSDAY
Where are you, my love? Where have the days gone of longing looks, and smiles meant for my eyes alone to see? I yearn so for the touch of your hand, if only to hold mine and walk along the park where you first told me of your love for me. Oh, Thomas, how I need you now.

FRIDAY
How do I tell you, dear husband, how much I need you here?
What is it that keeps you away from me? What is it that I have done? You are the light of my life, the strength

that helps me bear. Even with our babies, and Momma here with me, I feel so very alone when you are away.

MONDAY
You tell me that you love me. You say the words I long for. Yet, I cry to think that they have lost the passion that once pressed you to me. You have left me on my own to light the darkness. I am alone even when you are here.

"Emily," Addy's voice soared from the bottom of the staircase and swept through the closed door. "Emily, if you are up there, come down here this minute." It was a long staircase, one that Addy, with her aching joints, would let exact its price only when unavoidable. She waited as patiently as she could manage.

Emily slammed shut the journal, stood abruptly, and returned her secret where she had found it.

"Emily."

"I'm coming," she replied, closing the bedroom door behind her and testing her grandmother's patience by taking her time.

As Emily started down the stairs, Addy noted the deliberate avoidance of eye contact, the slow slide of Emily's hand along the mahogany rail. Halfway down, her patience ran out. "Have you been up there all this time? All the while that your sister picked and snapped the beans you were supposed to prepare for Mrs. Jameson?"

Emily replied with a silent stare, stopped her descent and sat down on the step.

"Your sister has done her own chores and yours many times over. Did you think that I didn't know?"

Still no response.

"Well, I do know. And I know why she's doing it and not complaining. She thinks that your momma left us because of you two fussing and fighting. I won't have you taking advantage of that, Emily. I won't have it. That had nothing to do with your momma dying."

Emily's eyes rose from their focus on the worn flowered stair-runner but still she said nothing.

Addy sighed, an audible white flag to the recent lack of responsiveness from her granddaughter. It was going to take time, and patience, she had no doubt of that. But, it tired her nonetheless. "You do your own chores tomorrow right after school," she said with a half a turn away. "Now, Miss Jenkins will be here in only a few minutes for your piano lesson, so come along."

"No," came the unexpected reply. "I'll not play the piano anymore."

"*Emily*," Addy said, now facing a defiant scowl. "Why on earth not?"

"Why should I? Papa won't be here. He doesn't care, why should I?"

"Your momma loved to play, and she was so happy that you were learning. You have a natural talent, Emily. Your mamma was so proud of you. And your papa is, too, even if he's not always able to tell you."

The defiant scowl deepened, becoming almost fierce if it hadn't been tempered by the tone of her young voice. "That's not true. He doesn't care about me or Anna. And he didn't care about Momma. *That's* why she wanted to leave, that's why she's not here with us now."

The ache that always started low in Addy's back, now crept across her hip and down the back of her leg. She stretched her hand out to Emily. "Come here, sweet child, come and sit in the parlor and talk with me. Things are going to be all right, you'll see."

The words had come as they should, said what should be and must be said. Yet, they held reservations, masking concerns that Addy wasn't sure she could hide for long.

"No," Emily said, as she rose from her seat on the stair. "It won't be all right." She pushed her posture forward, adding emphasis to her words. "You can't make it all right. You don't know what I know." She rushed down the last of the stairs, pushed away Addy's outstretched arm, and continued down the hall.

"Emily," Addy called, her voice more commanding now. "You stop right now and come back here." But her switch in approach made no difference. Emily had disappeared through the kitchen. The only response was the bang of the back screen door.

Like night and day they were, the girls, her girls now. She would raise them, of course she would, in the best way she could. Thomas's separation from the family became more apparent each day—days and nights spent in town, rare nights at home spent alone in his library. Unapproachable, inaccessible. And now, it was clear, even to the girls, no amount of hopeful discussion could change what his absence was proving.

7

It's probably wrong, Anna decided, how much being in Nessie's house, being with Nessie's family, made her happy. Emily would think it wrong. But then, Emily wasn't happy anywhere these days. Momma was gone, Papa didn't love us, and Grandma Addy wasn't going to tell *her* what to do—that seemed to be the sum of Emily's thoughts, at least those which could be deciphered from angry fits and long silences. The one thing that might have pulled the sisters closer seemed to have pushed them further apart. With Anna vowing to honor her mother's wishes, they no longer even shared fighting. They rode to school in silence, Anna tolerated Emily's daily criticism of Mrs. Jameson's cooking, and she had stopped complaining that Emily skipped out on chores.

It was evenings like this, in Nessie's tiny house packed with family, laughing and talking together, that made her want so much to be a part of it.

They squeezed around the old oak table that used nearly every inch of kitchen space and left only wiggle room behind the benches. Nessie's papa and grandpa took the chairs at the ends, while the boys and their grandma lined one side. Anna joined Nessie and her momma on the other.

A moment later the bustle of activity stilled, all hands were joined around the table and heads were bowed. Anna closed her eyes as Nessie's papa prayed. His voice, she was sure, could coax the very best of God's blessings on them all. Low, it was, and as smooth as warm honey. The sound of it wrapped around her, included her, asked blessings for her. Nessie's momma squeezed Anna's hand at the mention of her name. It was a good place to be.

The amens sounded all around, and the chatter began again as quickly as it had ended. John had fixed the broken tack good as new. Lewis was sweet on Mayme, and Jackson should mind his business. Grandpa Jameson would take the boys on Saturday to clear the fallen tree from the creek. And Nessie's momma and grandma would be fixing a special casserole for Sunday's social at the church.

"I wish Anna could come Sunday," Nessie said. "She's lettin' grandpa and me take the theater and puppets, so I can put on the show at the social. But it won't be the same if she can't be there to work Mavis. We did it just perfect today for the little kids."

Nessie's momma placed a piece of cornbread on her plate and spoke without looking up. "Some things just can't be, Nessie. But that don't mean we can't wish them different." She passed the basket of warm cornbread on to Anna. "I imagine you and Miss Emily will be expected at your own Sunday doing's," she said with a smile.

"Yes, ma'am," Anna replied, before facing the disappointment in Nessie's eyes. It was a look that struck directly, sending a sharp pain through her chest. She searched for a way to take it away, to make Nessie smile. "Nessie, let Lillie work Mavis. She will be so excited. She knows the story by heart, and she will think you are the best cousin in the whole world."

Nessie nodded, even smiled. But it was the closed, thin smile that signaled she knew there would be no further explanation. That was the end of it. It was time to eat, and to let the adults have their own discussion.

Their talk was punctuated by pauses taking the place of words that young children weren't supposed to hear, and looks that said things beyond the words they left out. But if children listen well enough they understand a lot of those, too. And Anna listened well.

"Joseph told me this morning there was another one right down the road from him last night," Nessie's papa was saying. "Heard the horses in the middle of the night. Got everyone hid. Didn't get no sleep at all. Still put in a hard day o' work today, though."

Grandpa Jameson raised his eyes to meet his son's. "What's it they say he did?"

"Nobody's sayin' yet."

42

"It don't matter," Lewis added, and his papa flashed him the look right away. But, being sixteen didn't mean that he had the good sense he needed. "They say he took a broken shovel handle from the trash behind the hardware store. Don't matter if he did nor not—"

"You calm yourself before you speak, son. And don't you ever talk like that outside this house. I've told you before—"

"It don't *matter*," Lewis shot back. "Maybe someone don't like what I look like. Maybe they don't like the way I laugh. Who's gonna stop 'em from beatin' *me*? Who's gonna stop 'em from *lynchin'* me? You? The police?"

Anna had never seen him look like that before. She'd never seen anyone look like that. The fear that should be there, like the fear in Nessie's eyes, and surely in her own, when the ghost moved the Billy doll's hat, wasn't there. Instead, Lewis's eyes sparked like a new log on a dying fire. The fear, wide-eyed and straight on, was in his papa's eyes.

"You listen to me," Nessie's papa said, his voice not as scared as his eyes, "and you listen good. Some men gonna find cause enough on their own. But me and mine ain't never gonna *give* 'em cause. You hear me?"

Lewis lowered his head, dropped his eyes to his half-finished meal. "Then who, Papa? Who's gonna—"

"It ain't your part to do it." Grandpa Jameson spoke slowly, with the calm his years had afforded him. "You were born of a free man, farmin' land that'll be your Papa's when I'm gone, and yours when he's gone. Them are the blessings you were born with," he said, jabbing the tip of a knotty finger on the table for emphasis. "Takin' care of them blessings," he said, "and the blessings you see in your momma's eyes, and your grandma's and your sister's, that's your part as a man." His gaze remained on his grandson, and he waited.

Lewis looked directly at his grandfather and nodded. "Yes, sir."

There was a settling, it seemed, at that moment, as the smells and tastes of dinner became a welcome distraction from the lingering tension. Dishes were passed about again, careful half-smiles tried to ease past the harshness. Nessie quickly grabbed the last two pieces of cornbread and gave one to Anna.

"Isn't it the best ever?" she asked, receiving a vigorous nod from Anna. "Momma made an extra pan for you to take home."

The chatter finally returned, overlapping itself, bumping and teasing, tones of trust and respect, the familiarity that Anna loved. She loved that it belonged to Nessie, that she could share it. And sometimes she imagined wrapping the feeling around herself like an old knitted shawl and taking it home with her. The only problem was that it never lasted long enough, slipping from her shoulders at the sight of the closed door to her father's den.

But for now, Anna hung on to the feeling and to Nessie's hand as they walked along the path toward home. They always walked each other halfway back, stopping at the break in the long line of piled rocks separating their familes' properties.

"Lewis said he's startin' out walkin' to the deep part of the creek at five o'clock, so you got to be ready 'fore that," Nessie said. "Once he gets settled on a fishin' spot, he don't want us makin' noise and interruptin'. We got to be ready if we want to go with him and do some serious fishin'."

Anna nodded, and hugged Nessie. "I'll have Grandma Addy wake me when she gets up. She's up groanin' before the rooster starts crowin'."

Nessie turned, hand in the air, to leave, but Anna stopped her.

"Hey, Ness?" Anna wore her most serious look. "That man, the one they lynched—if all he did was take something that someone threw out . . ." She looked at Nessie, waiting and knowing, then said the obvious. "What if it had been Lewis? It could have been Lewis, Ness, like when he found the piece of broken brass for the top of the puppet theater."

"He asked Mr. Barret," Nessie replied. "Told him what it was for."

"But, what if he hadn't? What if he had forgotten? What if no one believed him? You have to tell him, Nessie. Tell him as soon as you get home that he has to heed your papa's words. Please, Ness."

Nessie nodded, a quick dip of her head as she offered a hurried "okay," and turned for home. "Don't forget to get up early," Nessie called over her shoulder.

8

Tromping through the tall growth, a step behind Nessie, Anna felt her senses fully awakened in the cool morning air. She smelled the dampness of the moss and the wet, dark earth of its bank well before they reached the creek. Frogs plopped a noisy retreat at the unwelcome invasion.

The girls had been as quiet as possible, stepping through the knee-high growth and finding the clearing that Lewis swore was the best fishing in the whole creek. Since they never went home without a full string of smallmouths and spots, no one ever doubted him.

And no one doubted, either, that following Lewis's rules for fishing resulted in catching lots of fish. Except, maybe, the rule about baiting your own hook—"Because you can't be a real fisherman unless you do" never seemed to be clear enough reason.

Everyone knew their spot. Lewis and Jackson had made their way down the bank to a place above the large log that stretched across the width of the creek, so waterlogged now that it rested on the creek bed and the water rushed over it like a small waterfall. The boys liked to fish the water before the log, where Nessie's grandpa called the water "gin clear and just as smooth." But there was good fishing below the log as well. Nessie and Anna claimed their favorite places near the big bare branch that lay half in and half out of the water. The water pooled there in a deep, quiet pocket, and the girls pulled fat night crawlers from the can and threaded them onto their hooks. Accompanied by the sound of the water tumbling over the log in a soothing babble, they bounced their bait up and down in the pocket of water just as Lewis had taught them.

Anna pulled the back hem of her skirt up between her legs and tucked it into her waistband, then settled on the thick part of the log protruding from the bank. Nessie was smart: she wore a pair of Jackson's old pants. No one said "no," or told her how improper it was. It just made good sense. Anna never saw the boys' pants legs getting caught by grabbing branches, never saw the boys get their foot caught in a pant leg because they were running too fast and couldn't hold their pants legs up. Reason enough to have a good pair of hand-me-down pants.

There was a pretty good chance that she could get a pair of hand-me-down pants of her own from one of the boys. Grandma Addy and Emily wouldn't have to know. She could hide them easily in their little house, and wear them when it just made good sense. *Yes, it just made good sense. You can do a lot of contemplating when you're doing serious fishing. Much better than at night when worry and fear lay heavy on you, pressing your head beneath the pillow to try to shut them out.*

Lewis pulled the first fish of the morning from the creek. Even though he was sixteen, he still had a little boy smile—wide and toothy—the kind she saw on the little ones when they were by themselves and something pleased them.

Seeing that smile bought it back. Before she could stop it, that horrible feeling, the one that had started last night at dinner when she saw the fear in Nessie's papa's eyes. The vision of it and the feeling it gave her had kept her awake most of the night. She didn't want to believe that something so awful could happen to Lewis, but she had seen the belief in his papa's eyes. And she had seen a picture in a paper that Grandma Addy had tucked away behind her knitting basket. A lynching was not a proper picture for young girls to see. Anna had thought then that the man must have done something horrible, so horrible that only dying like that would pay for it. Now she wondered. Now she tried hard not to see Lewis' face on the man in the picture.

Something had changed that night at dinner. Something in the moment when she saw the look in Mr. Jameson's eyes altered her world in a way that even her mother's death hadn't. There was nothing final about it, like accepting death and knowing that you couldn't change it. No, she didn't feel hopeless like that. Instead, she felt nervous and jumpy, like she knew something she shouldn't. It had kept her awake all night, worrying that knowing that something bad could happen should also mean knowing what would stop it. And she didn't.

Sunday had been no better. Nessie had been gone all day at her church events, and Papa had brought them home immediately after church service and then left right away for town. He had no time anymore for playing horseshoes with the other men after church or helping to turn the ice cream crank for the socials. And nothing angered Emily more, lately, than not being able to stay and spend time with her friends. Last Sunday she had missed the social and a perfect chance to flirt with Jimmy Benton, and today she missed watching him play baseball. The fact that he wouldn't take notice of whether she was there or not, didn't seem to matter.

So with Papa off in town and Emily in a pout in her room, Anna spent the rest of the day weeding the front flowerbed, learning a chevron stitch from Grandma Addy, and thinking too much to her self.

She shared the love seat with her grandmother, practicing her new stitch on an old, worn pillowcase while Addy stitched together a new one. The song Addy was singing was "When You Were Sweet Sixteen," one that her Grandmother liked a lot. Anna knew the words and sang along sometimes. Tonight she mostly hummed—it was a good sound, like when Momma sang at the piano. It seemed like such a long time since she had heard her mother's voice.

She was glad that Emily was pouting in her room and glad that Papa wasn't there. Grandma was, too, Anna could tell. She never sang or hummed when they were around. And the way she was sitting was different, too: her shoulders were soft and relaxed instead of so stiff and straight. Maybe she needed everything to feel normal again, the way things were before Momma died. Maybe it's not so bad to want that. Normal.

It was comforting. Right now, looking at her grandmother, it was easy to make this her normal. Besides Nessie, it was the only part of her world that she could count on. Her grandmother had always been a constant in Anna's life, managing the ups and downs of the household—her mother's illness, her father's detachment, the friction with her sister. For as long as she could remember, Grandma Addy had filled the gaps, those spaces left wanting for security and answers. The spaces left by her father when he closed himself off from the family in his library and her mother when her eyes made no connection to Anna's world and held no promise of when they ever would again. So now, needing normal, she turned to her grandmother.

"Gram?"

Addy looked up from her work to survey Anna's stitches, more even now and consistent, and nodded in approval.

"Gram, did you ever know that something bad might happen to someone, but you didn't know what to do to keep it from happening?"

It was an unbalancing question, one that reached past the settled comfort of teaching and stitching. One with an answer that could strain the edges of her granddaughter's understanding, but Addy did not dismiss it.

"What has you so worried, child?"

The words tumbled out. "It's Lewis. He says things that make his papa scared. What if people hear him saying those things, and it makes them angry and they want to lynch him?"

Addy set her pillowcase aside and turned to fully face her grand-daughter. She spoke softly. "What things, Anna?"

"About Negroes getting beaten up and lynched, when they didn't do anything wrong. And Lewis's papa says if he keeps talking about it, he could get hurt, too. I told Nessie to tell him to heed his papa, but Lewis gets so mad, Gram."

"Sometimes," Addy began, "it's right to be mad. When things are unfair or unjust, when . . ." There was a lot that could be said, that really needed to be said, but how young was too young to understand the value of the risk? And, when the risk touched those so close, what then? The bell had been rung, and there was no denying that Anna had heard it clearly. A painful thing to witness, innocence lost. Worry and fear had taken its place, a heavy burden for such young shoulders.

"The best we can do," Addy continued, "is to treat others the way we want them to treat us. We can't keep all the bad from happening in the world. Sometimes we can't even stop it from happening to people we love."

It was a painful truth, one Addy knew firsthand. Hatred had stripped her of an irreplaceable love, taken away reason and hope, and left her with a secret she dared never reveal. For years, the same questions that were now beginning to worry her granddaughter, had haunted Addy mercilessly. Maybe there were no answers.

"But shouldn't we try, Gram? What if there is something that I should do, and I don't do it?"

What if I had known, Addy wondered, *if I had understood the hatred earlier, could I have changed the course of things?* A question, of course, too late to answer, too late for herself. But, for Anna, maybe a seed rightly planted, maybe some day there would be an answer.

"Sometimes," Addy began, "we don't know exactly what needs to be done, or what would help most to make things right in this world." Serious eyes waited for her wisdom, relied upon it. "But, as long as we know in our hearts what is right and what is good, we'll know what to do when the time comes." Addy covered Anna's hand with her own. "Lewis is a smart young man. He's been raised up to be honest and kind and respectful. He's growing up now to be his own man, and that means he'll have to know in his heart what is the best thing for him to do. No one can decide for him. He has to decide on his own and we have to respect that he will do what is right for him."

"But what if that means someone will want to hurt him?"

"He knows that's possible, Anna. He has to decide if fighting for what he believes is worth taking a chance on getting hurt. It's not up to us."

Addy watched Anna's eyes drop away. Not much of what she had

said was comforting. "It's all right to worry; it means that you care."
She patted Anna's hand. "And it's all right to stand up to others who
disrespect or wrong others. In fact, Anna, I expect you to."

"Even if it's a boy saying things?"

"Especially if it's a boy."

9

Only a sprinkling from Miss Whiting's morning lessons made it through the persistent anger that had Anna's focus glued to the back of Bobby Roberts' head.

It was a wonder that he couldn't feel the heat of her stare, burning like a hot iron poker into his skull.

There had been something even when he was younger, and not as outspoken, that had bothered her about him. She hadn't seen him steal something, or anything so singular that would have defined a less than acceptable character, but more a combination of things that made her avoid him whenever she could. He never let the younger kids play in the games with his friends, and he snickered loud enough for others to hear when someone gave a wrong answer during a lesson. And he smiled with his lips and not with his eyes, and talked over someone else's words before they finished. She didn't like him, but he wasn't someone she usually wasted much time on.

Until this year. Until, for some reason, he decided that being sixteen made it the right time to tell everyone what he thought about share-croppers and Methodists, and girls thinking that they are as smart as boys. It hadn't taken long for dislike to jump the gap to hatred. And that left Anna struggling with her mother's words that hatred was of the devil and did the most harm to those doing the hating. She was never sure how that worked, but she wasn't ready to say that her mother was wrong.

So, how did you not hate someone who said what Bobby Roberts had said this morning?

Anna was called to Miss Whiting's desk to accept this week's special book, extra reading she let Anna take home. All week she had waited

51

and planned how she and Nessie would read it together in their little house. And finally, there it was, sitting on Miss Whiting's desk.

But as she carried her treasure tucked in its canvas bag back to her desk, her happiest smile pushing her cheeks wide, Bobby Roberts had to ruin it.

"Stupid girl," he said in a loud whisper, as Anna approached his desk. "Have to take extra reading practice home."

Anna made no response. Instead, she gave him her best glare-eyes, narrowed and fixed for that extra moment in a direct challenge. When she returned to her seat the agitation quivered her innards far more than any argument with Emily ever did. He'd planted an instant doubt—caused her to wonder if he could be right and struggle with the hope that he was totally wrong. Left to her own unsoiled reasoning, she had no doubt of her capabilities or of the possibilities waiting for her in the world. But Bobby Roberts had a knack for soiling.

So she remained unfocused and bore holes through his skull until Miss Whiting excused them for recess. Then it got ugly.

Anna had no intention of confronting him, an older boy so full of undisputed answers. It wouldn't change his mind. It would only open up another opportunity for him to show his superiority.

No one had invited him and his two shadows to watch Anna and the other girls skip rope. And only Emily and Lillian, who always cared where the boys were, paid any attention to them.

"Lillian," Bobby said, "you sure skip a good rope."

Emily jumped in quickly to double with Lillian. Anna twirled one end of the rope and rolled her eyes.

"You, too, Emily," he said with a grin.

Anna could have taken the new book, gone off by herself to the bench by the woodpile behind the school and read. But that would spoil the chance to share the book fresh with Nessie and the thought made her stay with the jump rope. Putting up with the boys' unwelcome invasion meant that she and Nessie would be able to discover together all the exciting things the new book offered. And that was the way it should be.

So she twirled the rope and tried not to think about Bobby.

He wasn't making it easy, though. "Box social's Sunday," he said.

"Whatcha'll fixin'? Me and Pete and Tim gonna be decidin' which lunch to choose. My papa says Ruthie Baker and her momma fix the best chess pie in all Atlanta."

Lillian jumped clear to take Sarah's place twirling the rope. "My momma and me make the best chess pie this side of the Mississippi. We add cocoa powder."

"My momma said not to say what we're bringing," Sarah said. "You should leave it be a surprise."

"I'm not telling you, either," Emily added, stepping out to take the other end of the rope from Anna. "And, don't be askin' Anna. She'll be going fishin' with the Negroes."

Just the tone of her words made Anna cringe. Emily and her big mouth, spillin' personal business to the likes of Bobby and his shadows. It made her angry, it made her want to go back on her promise to her mother, but Anna held her tongue. She jumped into the twirling rope to take her turn.

"Fishin'?" Bobby's tone matched Emily's. "Fishin's not for girls, 'cept maybe nigger girls." The shadows laughed. "Your papa know you're fishin' with 'em?"

"Not your business," she replied.

"Sure is," he shot back. "There nigger boys hangin' around where you're fishin'?"

"No," she lied.

"'Cause that would make it my business, if you're so stupid to put yourself in harm's way."

Emily, for some unknown reason, let the lie stand. A rare thing that Anna would be grateful for something Emily did or did not do. But at this moment, she was grateful for sure.

Bobby, though, wasn't through. "I bet your papa doesn't know you're fishin'."

"Yes, he does." Another lie.

"Am I gonna find out you're lyin'? Cuz, if I do, I got no choice."

Was it something he saw in Emily's eyes? Or her sudden silence, so unlike Emily? Maybe her own reply was too quick, Anna thought, or too unsure. Whatever it was, something wasn't settling in Bobby's mind.

Anna stepped free of the rope. It stopped twirling. "What are you talking about?"

"Like my papa says, 'You gotta take care of them that are too stupid to know what's good for themselves'. If I found out there were nigger boys messin' around you, I'd likely take that rope there and go hang 'em myself."

What feminine reserve Anna had was gone. She charged toward Bobby, stopping no more than a foot in front of him. "Take it back," she yelled, arms rigid at her sides.

He seemed surprised at first, eyes wide, but recovered quickly. No one else moved. Only Emily spoke up.

"Stop it, Anna. What do you think you are doing?"

Bobby let a smirk be his first response. Then, "I'm not taking anything back."

"You've got no right," Anna continued, holding her stance, "talkin' big like you're somebody. Talkin' about hanging people who haven't done anything wrong."

"You got no right to tell me what to do," he said, pushing his face within inches of Anna's. "You're just a stupid girl."

The scale tipped. Anna slammed her palms against his chest, catching him off guard and pushing him to the ground on his butt. Without hesitation, she dove on top of him, her full weight behind her hands pinning his shoulders down flat, her face only inches from his. "Take it back!"

Only then did his shadows find their purpose. They grabbed Anna's arms and pulled her from their bewildered champion.

Emily wasted no time. "You're awful. You don't at all know how to act. I wish you weren't my sister."

"You're not Miss Perfect." Anna yanked her arms free and faced her sister. "You think you are, but you're not."

"Yeah, well, *you're* the one who is going to be in *so* much trouble when you get home."

The thought hadn't occurred to Anna, at the moment of impact with

Bobby Roberts's chest, that Grandma Addy's "stand up for what's right" advice didn't include physically leveling the offender. There was nothing to do now except pay the consequence, and remember to hold her anger in the future.

Trying to beat Emily in the door would have held no advantage, nor would it have stopped her from blurting her tattle over any explanation Anna attempted. So Anna held back, took her time gathering her books from the buggy, and looked to see if the signal board was up on the little house, while Emily raced to the steps and her chance to seal Anna's fate with their grandmother.

She expected the smugness on Emily's face. The disappointment, too, when Grandma Addy said, "Emily, take the laundry from the hall bench upstairs, please, while I talk to Anna." Poor Emily so wanted to hear that talk, but it would be left to her imagination.

Anna followed dutifully into the parlor and sat, as directed, on the love seat next to her grandmother. She met the familiar blue eyes, expecting a signature mix of disappointment and carefully controlled anger, but saw neither.

"Tell me what happened."

Anna offered her own version, honestly and apologetically.

And Addy nodded. "There will be times when anger, even when it is right to be angry, is not the right answer. And it isn't easy to turn that anger into something else, like an explanation of how you feel or what you think—even if you've said it before, and no one seems to care. Even if it seems that they will never change how they act or how they think, it doesn't mean that you should stop trying. And you know, many times, when you show your anger it only makes them more determined to stand their ground. Do you see what I'm saying?"

"Is it ever all right to hurt someone when you're angry?"

All right? Or, justified. When an innocent, loving soul is taken by ha-tred and jealousy? Oh yes, anger is justified. And putting an end to that hatred by denying it even one more breath on this earth? Yes, maybe that is all right.

"That's a question that even adults have a hard time answering, Anna. I don't know that I can answer it. I can only say that anger is

55

not reason enough in itself." How did you explain to a child a struggle that adults had yet to master? It should have been a simple thing: treat others as you want to be treated. Anger got displaced by understanding, and hate lost its hold to respect and tolerance. But it was a lesson taught to children and forgotten by adults.

Anna waited.

"Can you think of a better way to change his mind?"

"About girls being stupid?"

"I think that's a good place to start, don't you?"

Anna dropped her eyes to the books on her lap. She passed her fingertips over the title of the book she was so excited to share with Nessie.

"What if you asked Miss Whiting if you could report to the class about the famous women in the book?"

"Yes," Anna replied. "I'll ask her. She'll let me, I'm sure of it. And, that'll show stupid ole Bobby that girls are smart."

"Now, don't expect that he is going to admit he was wrong. But I'll bet that he will think about it some time when he's alone and maybe it will help him look at girls a little differently."

Anna nodded, placed the other schoolbooks on the table next to the love seat, and clutched the new book tightly to her chest.

"And perhaps," Addy added, "we should refer to Bobby Roberts as uninformed rather than stupid."

"Look, Nessie." Anna turned the page, as they lay together on the cot in their little house. They held the book between and read. "Joan of Arc."

Nessie read the information under the picture of the young woman in armor. "'Born a French peasant in 1412, Joan of Arc, claiming divine guidance, succeeded at the age of seventeen in rallying the French Army during the Hundred Years' War to defeat the British, paving the way for the coronation of Charles VII.'"

Anna responded in a reverent whisper. "Seventeen."

"Almost the same age as Lewis."

Still in awe, the girls went on to the next, and Anna took her turn to read. "'Clara Barton was born in 1821 and taught school for fifteen years prior to the War Between the States. With the onset of the War, she organized a service to get nurses and supplies to the army camps. She earned the name "Angel of the Battlefield," and was personally appointed by President Lincoln to search for missing prisoners. In 1881, Barton organized the American National Red Cross.'"

"The President himself sent her," Nessie said. "He must have thought she was very smart."

Anxiously they turned the page and read on. They read about Marie Curie and Florence Nightingale and Susan B. Anthony. They read in awe. Women were indeed smart, and they were brave and they did things that made a difference in the world. And, as the book confirmed, they were not all white.

Nessie's eyes widened. There it was, right there, clear as it could be on the page just below her picture. Mary Eliza Church Terrell, whose parents had been born slaves, attended Oberlin College, earned both a bachelor's and a master's degree, and went on to found the Colored Women's League in 1892. Nessie could barely take it in.

"Nessie," Anna exclaimed, "she's like you. Look, here's another."

And there on the very next page, another picture, a woman whose skin was even darker than Nessie's.

She'd heard the name, along with so many others, but never had Nessie seen their faces. "Harriett Tubman. 'Moses,'" Nessie said, "They called her 'Moses.' Right here, Anna, just like Miss Tilton told me. She helped lots of slaves run away to safety." She touched the picture as Anna read the accolades.

"What about Miss Ida Wells," Nessie asked. "She must be famous. Miss Tilton told me all about her, too."

Anna flipped a few pages ahead. "Yes," she said, "right here she is, Ness."

It made Nessie smile as Anna read from the book the very things that her teacher had told her about Miss Wells and the other Negro women who had done such wonderful things. There was always wonder in her teacher's voice, and a sense of possibility outside the familiar, the expected. And now, seeing their faces and their accomplishments there for anyone to read, they had become real beyond her imagination.

"Miss Whiting surely gets some fine books for us to read."

"Some, like this one, she says are best kept a secret. She said that some people would not think these are proper books for young girls to read."

"We will keep it a secret, won't we? And Miss Whiting will keep on sending the books for us. There must be so many books to read, and so many new things to learn."

"And when we're smart enough," Anna said, raising up to rest on her elbow, "what shall we become, Nessie?"

"A teacher," Nessie answered quickly. "Then we could have all the books we wanted and read them every night."

"We can be anything we want, Nessie. Maybe I'll be a nurse like Florence Nightingale, or write stories for newspapers to say how wrong it is to lynch people."

"Will we go to college like Miss Terrell?"

"Of course," replied Anna. "It'll be so exciting. We'll find jobs to do that people will pay us for, and we'll save our money."

"And we can't tell anyone what we're planning to do." Nessie sat up, too, and hugged Anna. "It's true, isn't it? We can do it."

"We can," Anna said, releasing their embrace and offering her hand. Nessie grasped it, right to right, and smiled. "You and me," they said. Left to left. "Best friends we." Arms locked tight. "Locked together, secrets forever."

10

Addy had yet to understand how this ambitious young woman, now sharing the parlor with her, had come to trust speaking to her without fear of reproach.

What on earth prompted her to have confidence in an old woman, to speak of things they both know to be outside society's strict and clearly defined boundaries? How could she have known what had never been spoken between them? Or, perhaps she did know that the boundaries had changed for Addy, once, years ago when the women took the reins left loose by war, and that some hadn't forgotten how that felt?

"Are we alone, then?" Leda Jenkins asked.

"We are," Addy replied. "Mr. Benson is in town, and it will be another hour before the girls are home from school."

Leda nodded. Dark wisps of hair, falling free of a pinned-up coif, fluttered with the air of the overhead fan. Large brown eyes locked with Addy's. "There has been another lynching. This one in Decatur. There's no justice to it, Miss Adeline, no proof of any wrongdoing deserving of death." Her voice flexed with a reserved strength. "It has got to stop."

"Yes, Leda, but I don't see what we can do to stop it. How do you know who you talk to by day, doesn't don a robe at night? You certainly know that even speaking of injustices has its own consequences." It was a question she had pondered often over the past year as she listened to Leda navigate the boundaries of discussions reserved for the men's club.

"But, it must start there. Don't you see? We must talk about it. Otherwise, what does our silence say? This is not only a Negro issue,

59

it's a human issue, it's our issue. It's not merely about justice for them, it's about our right as women to speak of it."

"Yes, but I'm afraid that it's a cause for others whose principles can weather the risks. Much of the care for my granddaughters is my responsibility. I'm all they have to count on. I can't risk *their* care and well-being for *my* principles."

Leda leaned forward, met the soft blue eyes and held their gaze. "I know who you are, Miss Adeline. I've listened to the talk; I've done my reading. I know who I am talking to. It was principle that saved this place, you alone standing against fear I can only imagine, facing Sherman's men eye to eye. There is no other way this house survived, except for your tenacious defense of principle."

"I'm not that young woman anymore, Leda. I'm old and I'm tired."

"And you want what is best for those girls. If there was a way to make this world a better place for them, I can't believe you wouldn't do it."

Addy's tone struggled to shed the years, to regain the stride of her youth. "Where is it you propose we speak about it?" she asked. "In meetings disguised with cooking and sewing and mindless chatter? Simply speaking to each *other*, none of us with the voice to change a thing? Even together, Leda, we are feathers in the wind."

"Together, you and I and every woman with a conviction of her own worth, have a voice that is stronger, and louder, and can reach the men who *can* make a change."

She couldn't deny it. Leda had stirred something in her that years of living, of merely managing and settling, had stilled. She saw in this woman's eyes what her own had once shown, heard in her voice the passion that had once powered her own words. But the years had also taught Addy the importance of the space between *should* and *could*. "There are too many men like my son-in-law who would fight hard to quiet us. There would be consequences. What of your husband? Do you jeopardize your marriage by speaking out?"

"I speak my mind at home. James has a sympathetic ear. He is a man of some compromise, but I do fear that if he is faced with standing apart from his peers, he would hesitate to support me. That's why we must find others, willing to listen, who are fundamentally *unopposed* to compromise. Men like James need to be able to find common ground. We start there." Leda grasped Addy's hand and squeezed it. "Help us search them out, Adeline."

So young, Addy thought, this woman—full of righteous conviction and hope. "Knowing that we are right," she said, "may be our only satisfaction at the end of a day."

"Then, we will add another day," Leda said, with a stiffening of her posture, "and another."

11

Everything had been thought out carefully. At special quilting meetings a certain amount of quilting actually did get done, not by the fastest stitchers, but enough to qualify in case someone from the regular quilting meetings became curious.

Six women stitched as though that was their true mission. They worked on their own quilt, made their own progress, and pursued their special mission. Their ages didn't matter, or their family name, or who their husbands were. What mattered was being there.

And they came armed. "Here's the article in the *Journal* for anyone who hasn't read it." Leda pulled the paper from her bag and passed it to Gladys Ashford, whose husband purposely kept the newspapers at work and out of their home. She had little doubt that the other four had read it.

"It's clear that the *Journal* is supporting Hoke Smith, although I doubt that Clark Howell would make any better of a governor."

Before anyone else could do anything but nod, Gladys quoted the article aloud, "'Howell appears to be unable to understand why it is that we wish the legal disenfranchisement of the 223,000 male Negroes of voting age in Georgia ...'" She looked up with the expression they had all grown to expect after her fresh exposure to news. "They're afraid Negroes will be able to actually vote."

"There is talk," Leda added, "that a number of Negro businessmen are uniting to vote in this election."

Margaret Houte spoke as she often did, with a peppery edge to her words. "Smith and Howell are each trying to outdo the other as to which of them will go the farthest to save us from Negro domination." Margaret's husband didn't keep all things political from her. But he didn't discuss them, either. He *stated*—his opinion, his fear, his anger. And she understood it, better than he knew. "Men are easily manipulated," she continued, "especially those who are afraid that voting will make Negroes think that they are equal to whites. That manipulation is what we should fear."

Addy had stitched, listened politely over the past weeks, and made her assessment. They were committed, these unassuming women, feeling their way in unsupported thought, testing a collectively unsteady voice. They spoke from conscience, felt its weight, and Addy saw in their eyes the heaviness of it. Addy had felt it, too, many years ago. Deeding land to Charles Jameson and paying a fair wage for Negro labor had gone a long way in lightening the weight. But it wasn't enough. She'd known it for a while: long before Leda Jenkins presented her with an almost unavoidable invitation to acknowledge it.

It was more than speaking out for a cause, more than trying to right a wrong—it was the speaking out, it was the voice. A collective voice, yes. But more, it was her own voice. She hadn't heard it, or claimed it beyond the boundary of her home in years. It had been too silent, too private, too self-absorbed for longer now than she could remember. The years, though, had not erased the memory of how she had let it soar once, for love, or how its strength of conviction had once made her feel. Leda was right. It wasn't just about the lynchings, it was about the voice.

"The papers are doing a fine job of that," Leda was saying, "manipulating. The *Constitution* is charging that Hoke Smith appointed Negroes to federal positions when he was part of Cleveland's cabinet."

"Inferring," Margaret injected, "that as governor he will also promote Negro status."

"Add to that the daily reports of Negro assaults against white women, and it isn't hard to see why people are afraid and angry."

"Do you think they are all true," Gladys asked, "the assaults?"

"It depends," Leda replied, "on your definition of assault. I have no doubt that there have been real assaults, by both Negroes and white men. But I also know that an article said that Mrs. Gates had been assaulted, when she told me herself that a Negro man had merely tripped and bumped against her arm. So, in some cases much is made of nothing."

Gladys had stopped stitching. "How are we to know, then, what to believe?"

Addy shook her head. "There is certainly enough cause for question. Lately, I've taken to reading the *Atlantic Independent*."

"A Negro paper?" Margaret asked.

"But, why not?" Leda added quickly. "I've been reading it, too. I want to know their perspective. The more information I can get, the better. We need to educate ourselves however we can."

"We can't approach politicians and men of influence with feelings and hearsay," Addy said. "Leda is right, we need to read everything, arm ourselves with as much information as possible, and approach them with a calm rationale."

"To talk about the lynchings," Margaret emphasized.

"I think initially," Leda's voice took on a tone perfectly suited to a political strategist, "we continue calling for the law to be applied fairly and equally, and emphasizing that injustice against some undermines justice for everyone."

"But who's listening?" Gladys asked. "Not men like my husband. He has forbidden mother and me to go to town without him. He would be furious if he knew that I was here."

"Your husband is a businessman, like my son-in-law," Addy replied, "and the growth of Negro-owned businesses is threatening them. They're going to support disenfranchisement in whatever form it takes. I'm sure that our letters have not met with any serious consideration. And the police chief has made it clear on a number of occasions that he is less than sympathetic."

"Then what do you think, Addy?" Leda asked. "Do we take the next step, go beyond letters and quiet meetings?"

"If we're serious about being heard, I think we have to use whatever voice we have. We could talk to businessmen face to face. It will be harder to dismiss our message if we make the effort to speak with them personally."

"Maybe Mayor Woodward would be receptive to sitting down and talking with one of us," Leda added, "especially if he is approached by a concerned citizen asking for his help. He *does* represent us, too."

Addy nodded. "I think you should be that concerned citizen."

12

The sound of the buggy returning behind the house captured Addy's attention. She stretched to see out the window from her stool at the kitchen table.

"Anna, see what it is."

Anna gladly left the silver and polishing cloth (her least favorite task), and went to the screen door to see. "It's Papa," she reported. "He and Emily are back from town already."

Thomas Benson helped his daughter from the buggy and marched ahead of her to the back steps, abandoning his one attempt in months to connect with at least one of his daughters. Anna opened the door and he rushed up the steps and into the kitchen. "What's Shackly's number?" he said on his way down the hall.

"One-thirty-seven," Addy replied, "What is it, Thomas?" Clearly something beyond the mundane for him to take on the task of calling the foreman himself. But he made no response and continued into the parlor.

Addy left her seat to meet Emily at the door. "What is it?"

Wide-eyed and pale, Emily replied, "We can't be in town today. Mr. Garrett met us before we got to Peachtree. He had closed his store and was headed home." She pulled the pin from her hat and removed it. "He told Papa to be a smart man and keep his family out of town today. He seemed so harried that Papa turned for home immediately."

"He never said what was going on?" Addy asked.

"He spoke so I couldn't hear the rest," she replied, as Thomas returned to the kitchen.

"I can't get through to the switchboard," he said. "Keep trying to ring him Adeline, and tell him to keep his family home. I'll ride down to his place in case you don't get through."

Addy grabbed his arm before he reached the door. "Tell me, Thomas, what's going on?"

"The Negroes, Adeline. They got everything stirred up real good this time." He turned to Emily. "It's nothing for you to worry over, Emily. You go do something that puts your mind to ease. I won't be long."

Emily nodded, leaned toward him, and gave a quick kiss to his cheek, then left the room without further discussion.

The screen door recoiled with a slap, and Anna, quiet until now, sprung to her grandmother's side. "Nessie," she said, her eyes demanding attention. "Nessie went to town with Little John."

"Go," Addy replied, "run and tell her family."

Anna bolted out the door, leaped clear of the steps, and ran full speed down the path through the field once tilled by Nessie's family as slaves.

It was a long run, but the thought that Nessie was in danger powered stride after stride until she reached the door of the little one-story house. It wasn't until she stopped to pound on the door that her quivering legs threatened to fold beneath her.

Willa Jameson opened the door to a breathless, frantic, and confused message. "You gotta get Nessie home, and Little John. Get 'em home. It's dangerous. Papa came home. It's dangerous."

"Take a breath, Miss Anna," Willa said. "You about to pass out. Come on in here. That's it. You take a breath and slow down."

Anna tried to catch her breath, grabbed her still quivering knees, and began again. "It's dangerous—"

"Sit down here," Willa said, guiding her to a kitchen chair. She pulled another chair close, settled on it, and took Anna's hand. "Slowly, Miss Anna, tell me slowly. What's dangerous?"

"Papa said that the Negroes have everyone stirred up in town." The fright pounding against Anna's chest now registered in Willa's eyes. "And, he said a smart man will keep his family home. He went to warn our foreman."

Willa nodded, rose without a word, and left the house. Anna followed her to the stalls where Nessie's father and brothers were working. She waited at the doorway as Willa calmly talked with her husband. A moment later, he was fitting a bridle over the nearest mule's head and pulling him from the stall. He ordered Lewis to saddle him, and met Anna at the door.

"Did your Papa say where the trouble is, Miss Anna?"

"No, only that they were stopped before they got to Peachtree."

"Calvin, wait," Willa said. "What if you're heading straight into a hornets nest? Little John's a smart boy. He'd stay clear if he saw a problem brewin'."

"But, if he didn't see it comin' . . . I can't see takin' that chance."

"What about the chance you're takin'? Who they gonna be more angry at, who they gonna claim's a threat? A bean-pole boy and a sliver of a girl that don't at all look her full age, or a full-grown Negro man?"

Calvin took the reins from Lewis and turned to mount.

"You know what I'm sayin', Calvin. You think on it."

"There ain't no thinkin' to it," he said, as the mule stepped forward under his mount.

Lewis started toward the stalls. "I'm coming with you," he said over his shoulder.

"You are not," Calvin replied. "You know what your responsibilities are. They're more important now than ever."

Lewis stopped short of the doorway and stood with his mother. "Yes, sir."

"You get the family to prayin'," Calvin directed to his wife, "and we'll all be home safe." With that, he prompted the mule and left his family to do as he said.

"Can I stay with you?" Anna asked.

"For a bit," Willa replied. "'Til time for your grandmother to start worryin'. One more child talkin' to the Lord just brings that much more blessing."

The walls of the tiny puppet store were covered with every manner of hand and string puppets. Little John slipped long, slender fingers under the loops on the board at the top of the puppet strings and lifted it free of its hanger. This visit to one of her favorite places had been Nessie's wish for weeks and Little John's promise. "Oh, look, Nessie," he said.

Nessie turned from a row of hand puppets to a jester in checkered pants and hat dancing awkwardly in front of her cousin.

"It even has a string for its mouth," he said, pulling a knotted end of a string with his other hand.

"That's a *real* fine puppet," Nessie replied. She took the puppet's legs in her hands and felt the structure beneath the fabric. "Can I try it?"

"Here," said the old puppet master emerging from his seat behind a wooden table. "Let me show you. That's a special one. Gonna take a little practice to make him sing and dance real fine."

He moved slowly, his back rounded at the shoulders, and made his way around the end of the table. He took the controller from Little John and showed them how to use the fingers of both hands to work all the strings. Then, under his mastery, the jester came alive on the floor between them. He bowed, tipped his head to the side, and asked, "Shall I dance for milady?"

Nessie smiled and nodded, and watched the nimble fingers make the jester move in a way that the old man could only remember.

"Here ya go," he said. "You give it a try."

He placed Nessie's smaller fingers in the correct positions on the controller and placed his own on top. "Follow me," he said, and lifted his fingers for Nessie to follow.

"Look at you, Ness," said Little John. "You've got him dancin' like a real puppeteer."

"Could I ever make him dance as good as you do?" she asked with a glance over her shoulder at her teacher.

"I believe you could, mmm-huh. You're gonna need a little practice, though." He smiled and nodded and straightened his back to its limit. "I'll tell you what. You come in here anytime you get a bit of time, and you can practice all you want."

"When can we come again, Little John?"

"Anytime it's alright with your momma."

It was perfect, her very own teacher, especially now when she had so many great ideas for making another puppet. Next time she would bring

Anna and after they got back home they would plan a whole new show. The thought jumped with anticipation until it was interrupted by a young man about Little John's age bursting through the door of the shop.

"Mr. Davis," he said with apparent urgency. "Mr. Herndon from the barbershop sent me. He's closin' up and gettin' home. He says you got to do the same." He turned to Little John. "You, too. You best be leavin' outta the business district. There's a big mob of white men pullin' Negroes off the trolley at the end of Peachtree and beatin' 'em. Git some place safe," he said, leaving through the door as quickly as he'd entered.

The old man hesitated only long enough to place the puppet back on its hanger. "What direction is home?" he asked of his customers.

Little John pointed and replied, "Brownsville."

"Git along, then. And do as he said, stay away from the trolley."

"You're lockin' up, aren't you? Do you need any help?"

"Just gotta git the lights. Go on, git goin'."

Little John nodded. "Come on, Ness."

The door locked behind them, and the shop went dark by the time they had crossed the street. Herndon's barbershop was indeed closed, locked and dark, but another on the other side of the street was still open. It was an odd mix all along the block, some businesses open, others closed up tight.

The normal, familiar sounds of the city, the clatter of the trolley along its track, horses hooves clacking over the bricks, and the mixed hum of distant conversations had been replaced with an eerie quiet. A collective hold of a long breath, waiting for an unknown release. They moved quickly along the streets, eyeing dark spaces between buildings cautiously and hurrying their steps past them. It was the shortest and most direct route to Brownsville, but it meant coming within a block of Five Points before turning for home.

The small group of white men who had started gathering earlier in the day at Five Points near the center of town now counted in the hundreds as word of more attacks spread through the saloons and businesses. All morning and into the afternoon, the newsboys had shouted their high-pitched headlines. "Extra! Bold Negro Kisses White Girl!" from one corner. "Third Assault on White Women in Two Days!" from another.

Liquor and a growing sense of self-appointed justice fueled the responses. "Who's protecting our women?" Anger gained momentum— "The police do nothing"—and made the decisions: "Let's take care of it ourselves."

The tenor and agitation forced Negroes to stay inside the shops, or avoid impending danger by escaping to the police station a street away. They pleaded their case, refused to leave until officials made a move.

Mayor Woodward, flanked by officers, and police commissioner James English, worked their way to the head of the crowd at Five Points. He bumped and pushed his way through. "All right," he yelled. "Listen to me!" He held his arms up high. "Listen to me!" He knew these men, some by name, some by family, most because they were just working men like himself. He understood them—angry and frustrated. But he wanted nothing like this exploding into something that would be caught by the papers up North and do damage to his city's fine reputation.

He lifted his voice again, attempting to be heard over the rumblings. "I'm asking you to go on home, and stay off the streets. Let Commissioner English and his men handle the Negroes." The rumblings quieted for a moment. "The honor of Atlanta before the world is in your hands tonight."

"Nigger lover!" came a drunken response. "You're just a nigger lover!"

"Police ain't doin' nothing," shouted another, a prompt for parroting shouts and agreements.

Then the declaration that united them, "We'll take care a them niggers ourselves."

"Let's go get 'em," was the cry that broke the dam, and the sea of angry men moved at once, flooding down the streets from the Points.

Little John and Nessie were close enough now to Five Points to hear the shrill of a newsboy filling the evening air with more fuel for the mob. "Extra! Third assault on white women by Negro brutes!"

They could hear the men before they saw them, shouts of anger echoing along the block of taller buildings. Little John grabbed Nessie's hand to stop her next to him. "We can't go this way, Ness. There they are."

He turned abruptly, pulling Nessie with him. "Come on, we have to go the long way, back to Wall Street." He let go of her hand and started to run.

He didn't have to tell her to keep up, to run her fastest and not get separated from him. She knew. His eighteen-year-old legs had nothing on her younger ones. Her heart pounded so hard that she felt it in her throat before she had even started to run. She heard the sounds, if not the words, of the danger behind them—guttural bursts, breaking glass, shrieks of fear. And she knew that if they didn't run fast enough, the sounds would overtake them and it would be painful, terrifying and painful. It wouldn't matter that they had done nothing wrong, that they went to church on Sundays, that Little John freed dragonflies from spider webs. It just wouldn't matter.

Calvin Jameson pounded his fist on the door of his brother-in-law's house. Adrenaline and worry left no room for temperance. When no one answered, he pounded harder. Only when desperation caused him to shout, "John, Lilly, it's Calvin," did he see the drapes move in the front window.

The door opened and his brother-in-law greeted him with a slide action Winchester.

"Nessie," Calvin blurted, as he stepped inside. "Is she here?"

"They aren't back yet."

The news turned Calvin around toward the door, but John caught his arm and stopped him. "We need to wait here," he said.

"That's my baby girl out there, John. It's too dangerous."

"Yes, it's dangerous, but even more for you and me. We've got to

72

be sensible here. Actions got to come from our heads, not our hearts."

Sensible was exactly how John Carver had come to own his own profitable insurance company, and how he and his family had become part of the growing number of Negro middle class. He was smart, had an eye for the future, and cautious. He was—frustratingly—right.

"I know as well as you do," he continued, "how hard it is to wait, and trust." He relaxed his grip on Calvin's arm when it was apparent that his message had taken. "Lilly and the neighbors are safe in the cold storage. You and I will stand vigil here."

Calvin responded with a reluctant nod. "There's times when sensible just don't seem right."

"I know that to be true," John replied, pulling a chair from the dining room close to another at the window. "That I do." He left the light in the dining room on, and the one near the door off. They settled in the chairs, out of view from the window and waited.

Calvin didn't settle well. He shifted about, leaned forward, then back. "What good sense would have let them go today?"

"The same sense that let them go all the other times."

"But the newspapers and the governor's race . . . I just had my head down, believin' it had nothin' to do with me and mine. I never should have let Nessie come to town." He shook his head. "Where all would they have gone?"

"He took her to the theater, and then they were going to some shops on Peachtree. Little John knows to stay away from Decatur Street."

Calvin stood. "I have to go after 'em." He moved to the door quickly and unlocked it.

John bolted from his chair and pushed Calvin from the door.

Surprised, Calvin replied, "Bein' family don't give you the right to tell me what to do." He firmed his stance.

"No, it gives me the right to care about your family the same as mine." He stood defiantly between Calvin and the door. "You're not making my sister an early widow. You'll have to knock me out to get out this door."

Calvin raised his arms out to his sides and shook his head in passive defiance.

Without warning, the door slammed against John's back and sent him falling into Calvin. Bursting through the door came a breathless Little John with Nessie on his heels. John caught his balance, slammed the door shut and locked it.

"Are they coming behind you?" he asked.

Little John collapsed on a chair. "I don't think so," he managed.

"They couldn't run as fast as us," Nessie said, as her father grabbed her in a tight embrace.

"Faster than a trolley, easy," Little John added.

John grasped his son's head and pressed it to his side. "Good that you're both safe." He released his grip and asked, "Could you tell where most of the trouble is?"

"Seems like it started at Five Points, but they were comin' behind us on Peachtree, breakin' windows and beatin' people."

"Mr. Smythe next door said there was a big crowd of Negroes taking a stand on Decatur," John said. "He closed his office on Auburn. Word was that the crowd of whites was huge, and nobody could tell where they would go. He didn't want to take a chance, and came home. He's worried that with so many Negro business owners living here, that they'll target Brownsville."

He picked up the rifle and handed it to John. "He could be right. It's best you not try to go home tonight. Little John, take Nessie to the shelter, and tell your momma to keep everyone there 'til we come get them. And bring me back Grandpa's old rifle."

Nessie sat next to her aunt on the rough wooden bench. Lilly wrapped her arms around her and spoke in hushed tones. "Don't be scared. You're safe here with us." Hushed was the rule, Little John made sure she knew. And, if the bell in the cold storage jingled, it was candle out and total silence. The elderly couple from next door shared another small bench, close enough in front of them that their knees nearly touched.

Nessie watched them, sitting still and calm despite the danger. They met each other's eyes, then dropped their focus away without a word between them. She wondered how old Walter Smythe and his wife were. Wondered if they had had to run as slaves or if they had stayed put wherever they were until they were freed. She wondered what they were thinking.

The tiny area, with its earthen floor and cobweb-draped floorboards overhead, bulged from a tunnel half its height. Little John had told her the story—escaped slaves slipping from the shadows of trees now gone, to the Smythe house barn where they found food and water, then dropping through the hole beneath the hay bales to follow the tunnel to the little room where Nessie huddled now.

Now, forty years past its intended use, it offered safe hiding still—needed, still. How scared they must have been, Nessie thought, waiting, listening for the bell. Two for danger; four, safe to run. Did their hearts pound as fiercely as hers had tonight, their legs push way beyond their strength for fear of failure? And if they did fail? She'd heard the stories, the ones watered down for young ears, and read the ones that weren't. She knew what happened when an escaped slave hadn't made it to a place like this, or to the next. They were sad stories, sad, and Nessie never doubted their truth. But they had never touched her life like this.

Not once had the long ago wrongs caused her worry or fear. Stories of the past were left there. Her family was free and safe. Hard work brought them what they needed and kept them together. She couldn't see any of that changing. Until now. Until this space, pungent and dark, whispering its history to her and hiding her just as it had them.

Nessie welcomed her aunt's embrace, the gentle rocking and low hum of favorite hymns resonating against the top of her head.

Walter Smythe held his wife with one arm around her shoulders. She held his other hand in both of hers. Both had said very little—a silent waiting. No nervous conversation, with that hopeful lilt that made you worry even more because you knew that they were trying to convince themselves. Only a strange calm, and a kiss that lingered at his wife's temple. Nessie watched them and tried to understand it. Maybe they knew something that she clearly did not—like how tonight might end, or why. It seemed as though that kind of calm should be reassuring, but it wasn't. Reassurance radiated from the arms around her and from the soft melodic sound of her aunt's

75

voice. Nessie began counting the number of times Mr. Smythe patted his wife's shoulder—pat, pat, squeeze. The same pattern, repeated. Minutes later, again. His way of reassurance. Nessie's way of moving time.

The big house was still, except for the faint chime of the old clock in the parlor marking the half hour. Anna slipped quietly partway down the stairs, stopped, and peered over the banister to the parlor door. A soft light spilled from the doorway into the darker hall. Everyone should be sleeping. But for Anna, sleep wasn't possible. She went the rest of the way down the stairs and approached the parlor.

The sound of the phonograph was barely audible. Grandma Addy sat close by, leaning heavily on the arm of the love seat, her hand resting on the phone box on the table. She was still dressed in her day dress and shoes, her hair still pinned up on her head. When she noticed Anna in the doorway, she held out her hand.

Anna padded barefoot across the thin wool rug, gathered her nightgown, and settled next to her grandmother. She tucked her feet beneath her and nestled against Addy's side. "Have you heard anything about Nessie?"

"Nothing yet. The switchboard has been jammed up all day. And Little John's family is on a different company line . . . but sometimes not hearing anything only means that there isn't anything to hear."

"You're worried, though, aren't you? Just like me."

"Worry won't do much to help, I'm afraid," Addy replied.

"I love Nessie, Grandma. I couldn't stand it if she was hurt."

"I know, child, I know."

"Can you call someone? Can you try again?"

"It's getting so late," replied Addy. "But maybe we could get a line." She picked up the phone and waited. "Yes," she said after a few seconds. "Yes, thank you. Can you put me through to Leda Jenkins, one-ninety-three." Then, moments later, "Oh, Leda, I've tried to get someone all day. What is happening in town? We have people there and we're worried."

Anna listened intently, but the I sees and yeses from her grandmother told her nothing.

"Yes, we'll meet here," Addy replied. "Ring me tomorrow, and we'll decide when. Thank you, Leda."

"What did she say? How will we know if Nessie's all right?"

"It sounds like things have calmed down for tonight. But, there's no way to know about Nessie right now. Try not to worry. I'm sure that they will be coming home as soon as they can. You go on to bed. I'll stay and watch for them."

"I tried, I can't sleep." She turned and reached behind to open the drapes on the window facing the road. "Please let me stay and watch with you. Please, Gram."

Addy patted her granddaughter's knee. "We'll watch together," she said as she rose. "You get comfortable." She settled in the rocking chair more directly facing the window, and they began their vigil together.

Time, kept audible by the grandfather clock on the far side of the room, crept at a pace suited only for happy times and savored moments. The sound of it mocked Anna's impatience. Her questions didn't help, there were no answers. Her grandmother's attempts at reassurance proved only how helpless the two of them were. Time would tell it, the good or the bad, when God saw fit to make it so. That was all either of them knew.

The sounds of the house, the quarter-hour chimes, the slow creak of Addy's chair, usually sounds of comfort, were drowned by the blare of Anna's thoughts. *What if the men had grabbed Little John and beaten him, or worse? What if Nessie saw it? Quiet, gentle Nessie. How scared she would be, how hard her heart would be pounding, wanting to help him but knowing she couldn't. What would she do? Run. Surely she would have to. And if they caught her?* Why had she read the stories tucked away where she wasn't supposed to find them? The horrible things they said happened to slave girls, they wouldn't happen to Nessie. They couldn't happen. But, the possibility of it wouldn't leave her thoughts.

Rain, light in the early part of the evening, now beat steadily on the porch roof. Anna glanced again at the clock, just short of the two-thirty chime. She wondered if she would hear the buggy. Clouds obscured the light of a nearly full moon. Could she even see it?

"She's gonna be all right, isn't she, Gram?" She hadn't intended to say the words out loud, again. Her thoughts repeated themselves too many times to voice them. Quiet worries with no answers had just grown too loud.

"Let's think the best, Anna," her grandmother's expected reply. "It's all we can do."

Yes, will good thoughts, and watch.

Anna was doing just that when she heard it—something beyond the rain. She pressed close to the window, cupped her hands on either side of her face to block out the dim light of the room. Yes, there was movement on the road, and clearly now the sound of a horse trotting closer.

"It's them!" Anna exclaimed, jumping off the love seat. "I know it is."

Addy rose from the rocker as Anna raced from the room. "Anna, your shoes."

But her words were lost on Anna racing to the back door, and out into the night. Bare feet slapped through puddles and down the drive toward the road.

"Nessie! Nessie!" Anna shouted her name louder than she had ever shouted. "Nessie!"

Less than halfway down the drive, she could see the buggy turn off the road and onto the drive.

Calvin Jameson brought the buggy, with the mule tied behind it, to a stop beside Anna. "Get up here in the buggy, Miss Anna. Your grandma know you're out here this time a night?"

Anna scrambled into the buggy, and grabbed Nessie in a tight embrace.

"Did you stay up all night?" Nessie asked.

"Me and Gram both. I was so worried, Ness."

The buggy lurched forward. "I'll get you back to the house. You get dried off and tell your grandma that we are all fine."

The words spilled naturally. "It was really scary. Little John and I outran 'em. I ran as fast as him. And, we hid under a cold storage where—"

"Nessie, Miss Anna don't need to hear about that," Calvin interjected.

78

"She needs to get in the house and get some dry clothes on." He stopped close to the back steps, and Anna hugged Nessie once more before climbing down.

Standing in the light of the back screen door, Addy called, "Is everyone all right, Mr. Jameson?"

"Yes, ma'am," he replied. "We're fine. You needn't have waited up like that."

"I wouldn't have done much sleepin' without knowin'."

"Then, I thank you, ma'am. I'll be gettin' my girl here home, so her momma can see for herself. You can rest easy."

13

The women gathered around Addy's dining room table. There was no pretense of quilting today, only a palpable sense of urgency. Leda took her place at the end of the table.

"Nessie and her family are safe?" she asked.

Adeline replied from the other end of the table. "Yes. They traveled past midnight in the rain."

"It seems Mother Nature was able to control what the police could not," Leda said. "But, I'm afraid it was temporary. The crowds have gathered again. We passed National Guard troops on our way out here."

"I didn't think we would be able to meet," Margaret said. "With all the chaos, I expected to be told that it was too dangerous. Thanks to you, though, Adeline, coming out here was considered a safer place to be."

"Even my husband," added Gladys, "didn't question my leaving."

Leda leaned forward on the table. "Women's work will keep you busy and safe. Let him think that for as long as you can. But, for our real work," she directed toward Addy, "we need new direction."

"The riot has certainly changed things," Addy replied. "I did a lot of thinking while we waited for word of our friends' safety. You all know that I've advocated for caution, and there is still need for that. But it's clear to me that using our voices to influence men just isn't enough to make the changes that we want. I think that we need to join the women of the Equal Suffrage Party."

"Adeline's right," Leda added. "There is power in numbers, and our fight now must be to gain our own voice."

Margaret nodded. "Our voices and our opinions are constantly being filtered and censored. We have to put our efforts toward the vote if we are going to have any power."

There were nods around the table, except for Gladys. "I can't be involved with an organization like that. If my husband even knew what we talked about at our quilting meetings ..."

"There's need for both," Addy said. "There is a lot of influencing that has to be done if we are to get the vote. You continue to talk with your women friends at church. Convincing them that their opinions are important can go a long way in changing social attitude in our favor."

And Leda added, "We can continue our quilting meetings. Those are the only times that we can support each other and be able to explore new ideas. Each of us has something important to offer."

It was more than the message of their words that kept Anna sitting on the floor outside the dining room, listening. She hugged her knees and leaned her head against the wall. She loved the sound of their voices, the way each lifted up another. She imagined being among them, the voices speaking to her, making her feel important, worthy.

Her grandmother was not alone. The things that were important to her, the lessons and feelings that she had given Anna, were the very same things that they were giving each other. Lessons, she realized, that were bigger and more powerful than she had imagined. Anna wanted what these women wanted. She wanted to live in the world they envisioned. She wanted to be wise like her grandmother and strong like Leda. And she would sit right here and listen for as long the women stayed. Next time, she would find a way to join them.

PART II
1917

14

There was lightness about the day, about this Saturday in town with Momma, an easiness that Nessie noticed more today than any other since the beginning of their once-a-month routine.

It had been almost a full year since they lost Grandma Jameson to a 'flu outbreak that had threatened most of Nessie's family. She had given them her days and her nights, cleaned them and comforted them. She'd forced water to even the most reluctant, and cooled their bodies with rags soaked in well water until their fevers broke. And it wasn't until they'd regained their strength and made it through that her grandmother's own weakened body lost its fight. With one long, soft sigh, she settled her thin frame onto the warn grey cushions of the sofa, laid her head back and closed her eyes, and never opened them again.

Such a quiet presence, her grandmother, yet evidence of her absence was everywhere—still. Absent was the morning greeting that had always started Nessie's day. "There's my sweet child," she would say as Nessie smiled, "puttin' the bright in my day." Gone, too, were the special times when growing, demanding boys dominated her mother's time, and her grandmother slipped in with a sly wink and whisked her away. It was their special, tucked-away girl time. Times for Nessie to learn of her family's journey, their struggles and their triumphs. Through her grandmother, she better understood her grandfather's resolve to quietly hold his place, to lower his head and appreciate what was. She was beginning to understand her father's anger at his own fear. An anger, seemingly directed at what her grandmother called civil disobedience, that did not come from submission, but from the strength to do whatever necessary to protect his family. She could see that now. It was that same control that he wanted desperately for her brothers to have.

There was so much more that Nessie wanted to know, so much more that her grandmother could have taught her. Now there would be only memories struggling to fill the spaces that had belonged only to her grandmother. The sadness of it sometimes overwhelmed her. But not today.

With her aunt too lame to go to town, today was Nessie's day with her mother. No boys to keep in line, no other adults to monopolize the conversation, it was just the two of them.

They made the usual rounds, replenishing staples at the mercantile, dropping off laundry, clean and folded, to Mrs. Shelby, a shut-in now, and leaving the mule and wagon at the blacksmith's to have a piece made for the mule's harness. At each stop they exchanged smiles and cordial greetings. Friends stopped them in stores and the middle of the walk to talk. For the first time, Nessie felt a sense of belonging, of acceptance beyond her family, beyond her church.

That is until they entered the white-owned mercantile. "They have a much larger selection of yarn," promised her mother. "We'll find the color you need to finish the wedding blanket there."

Her mother's demeanor had changed the moment they left Auburn Avenue and the block of Negro-owned businesses. There was no further conversation. They traveled the street side of the walk with their focus straight ahead. There were no nods or smiles, only an air of otherness that grew to stifling just inside the store.

On the days when old Jona had driven them to town, she'd watched from the buggy as Anna breezed in and out of this store, sending happy thank yous over her shoulder. But this was different, and Nessie knew it.

Two white women, looking about the age of Nessie's mother, set their merchandise on the wooden counter and chatted with the man behind the register. Nessie pulled a piece of yarn from her pocket and followed her mother to the cubbyholes on the wall filled with more colors of yarn than she had ever seen.

"Look here," her mother said, holding two different skeins next to Nessie's piece. "This is the one, right here." She smiled and reached to put the other skein back in its place. As she did, the large brim of a hat creased her cheek, and a woman reached across her, knocking the skein from her mother's grasp.

Willa Jameson backed up, touched her cheek with her fingertips, and pulled Nessie back beside her. They waited silently. The woman made her selections, and took them to the counter, before Willa picked up the skein from the floor and replaced it. They kept their distance while the woman made her purchases.

"Will this be it today?" the man behind the register asked her. "Or, is there something else I can help you with?"

"This will do for now," the woman replied. "Thank you."

He smiled. "Then, that'll be three skeins, at ten cents each, for a total of thirty cents."

The woman counted out the coins and placed them on the counter.

"Thank you, ma'am," he said with a nod and a smile. "You have a nice day now."

Before another customer entered, Nessie stepped forward and placed the skein on the counter, and opened her coin purse.

"Fifteen cents," the man said.

"But, you said—"

"I have it, Nessie," her mother said, quickly placing the money on the counter. "We are truly grateful that you had just the color we need." She nudged Nessie with her elbow.

"Yes, sir," Nessie complied, "we are truly grateful."

The man said nothing, merely deposited the coins in the register and watched as the two women left his store.

They walked in silence, and headed back toward the blacksmith shop. As they rounded the corner, movement behind the mercantile caught Nessie's attention. She turned instinctively to see what it was, and the sight surprised her. There, tucked behind the open back door, was Emily, oblivious to all else except the tall young man with his arms wrapped around her. Emily, the proper one, always ready with an exposé of what must be, now in clear contradiction of her own moral code.

Nessie snapped her attention forward, and quickened her steps. With a touch of luck, Emily wouldn't see her, and Momma wouldn't see Emily. There was only one person who needed to know what she had just seen, and that was Anna. And there was only one reason she needed to know, a future need for protective ammunition. With Emily, it was always important to have something held in reserve, and this was huge. Nessie nearly giggled out loud at the thought.

She fought the urge until they neared the blacksmith's, and her mother's tone immediately expunged her giddiness.

"What was in your mind, Nessie? You know to hold your tongue."

Just that quickly, her mind was returned to that stifling air of the mercantile, where her mother's thoughts clearly remained. "But, why should we have to pay more, Momma? And why is it okay for that woman to treat you so rudely?"

They reached the front of the wagon, and Willa turned about sharply. "Just what makes you speak like that?" Willa replied. "You were raised knowing that some things just must be."

"But it isn't right, is it?"

"We can't be thinkin' on the right or the wrong of it. That kind of thinkin' only breeds trouble. Miss Tilton been puttin' notions in your head? She been givin' you Miss Well's writin's to read again?"

"What's wrong with people wantin' to make things better?"

"People don't see the risks. Your papa's kept this family safe by bein' grateful for the blessings we got."

"I know, Momma. But what if everyone had settled for bein' grateful for the good things and kept on toleratin' the bad? How would we have ever—"

"By trustin' in the Lord, Nessie, and workin' hard. Now, get yourself in the wagon."

Nessie climbed onto the seat and took the reins, but she wasn't ready to give up her opportunity to speak her mind. As soon as her mother was settled and the mule eased into a gait, Nessie continued.

"But, if the Lord said, 'Let he who has not sinned cast the first stone', and the Bible says that all men are sinners, then what makes it right for a white person to treat Negroes like we're not worthy? Or, why is it that a man is more worthy than a woman?"

"'Worthy'? Nessie, why do you say 'worthy'? You've been raised up to know your worth. Can't nobody take that from you."

"They can," Nessie replied with a conviction she knew would give her mother pause. "They can strip it away as fast as it takes to push you aside or call you a name."

"What happens on the outside don't matter, that's what you got to remember. It's what's in here," she said, patting her hand over her heart, "and in here," she placed her index finger against the side of Nessie's head. "That's what holds you up strong, and knowin' that you got the respect of your own."

"But, what if I want—"

"No more talk on it. We'll take Aunt Ellie's goods on to her and share a bit of lunch. We'll have a nice visit."

End of discussion, if you could call it that. Nessie knew that pressing further would not change her mother's convictions, not today. So for now, she would have lunch with her aunt, listen to the latest family gossip, and tolerate the inevitable.

"Now, when you gonna git serious about some nice boy?" her aunt will say, zeroing in on Nessie's eyes until there was no avoiding her.

The answer will be the same as always. "I guess I've been so busy, I haven't had time for boys." And then the attempt to talk about something, anything else will disappear into the void between them, and Aunt Ellie will continue the torture.

"You'd better git busy all right," she'll say, followed by a girlish giggle. "Now, Willa, you got to give your girl some time offa those chores, and start invitin' some of them boys from church to come around."

Which wouldn't be a concern right away. Lewis's wedding will be enough to occupy Momma's thoughts for a while. But after that, serious dodging maneuvers would be important. Something Anna was already getting pretty good at.

15

"Love," Pastor Emmons said, his hands folded gently across his black robe, his eyes resting on the young couple before him, "is the greatest gift our Lord has given us. And the greatest gift we can give each other."

The white clapboard church with its old pine benches was filled to capacity. Lewis stood facing his bride, his smile so wide he could barely form his vows. Friends and family bore witness on this special day, all except Grandma Jameson. And so, this day, his grandmother's birthday, was the one Lewis had chosen to start his new life. A fitting tribute, to be sure, for the sacrifice she had made.

As Pastor Emmons neared his closing, Nessie turned in her seat and stretched to send a smile to Anna sitting in the back row with Grandma Addy. Nessie's momma grasped her arm with a "just a little longer" message, and Nessie refocused.

"You have chosen each other," Pastor continued, "to receive that blessed of all gifts. And I, through the power granted me by our Father, pronounce that you are now husband and wife. Lewis, please kiss your beautiful bride."

Everyone stood as the happy couple almost ran down the aisle. Nessie grasped her momma's waist, and pressed her forehead against the back of her momma's shoulder. She stifled the impulse to shout it out loud. "Oh, Momma," she said, barely controlling her excitement, "they look so happy, don't they?" She looked quickly to the back of the church, where Anna's smile mirrored her own.

"The new Mr. and Mrs. Jameson," the Pastor began in announcement tone, "would like you to join them in celebration of their new life together at the Graysons' at Springhill. The Lord is surely smiling today."

The celebration was in full swing under the big white tent. Everyone was in Sunday best, food fit for royalty covered the plank tables, and Little John's musician friends had young and old dancing as if there was no happier moment in the whole world.

Today, the tent was set on the west side of the house, nearest the big tree. Children squealed and laughed in the shade of the massive branches, and "proper" was an unnecessary thought.

Grandma Addy lifted her cartwheel hat, with its layers of white lace, and placed it on her lap.

Beside her, Willa Jameson surveyed the festivities. Her wide-brimmed hat, and its hand-sewn orange and white lilies, was still perched proudly on her head. "It is a party to behold, yes it is," she said.

"That's a fine woman your young man has found. Anna speaks highly of her."

"She's as smart as they come. The kind of woman who can talk to a man, make him see the right through the wrongs. Help take some of the worry off my heart."

"We come by worrying the natural way, Willa. We want what is best for our children, and our grandchildren. And when that time comes that they're making life's decisions on their own, all we have left is the worrying."

Willa nodded, watching a growing group gather to dance to a new ragtime tune. "Don't seem that I'll have half the worries with Jackson. He's always been such a quiet boy."

Addy smiled. "Ah, but then we have the girls, don't we? A whole different set of worries there."

"That we do," Willa said, and added a soft little laugh. "That we do."

"Come on, Anna," Nessie said, grabbing Anna's hand and pulling her to the edge of the group at the far end of the tent. "I'll teach you the cakewalk. It's so much fun. Little John taught me. Come on."

The music had taken a decidedly livelier turn shortly after the pastor and his wife left to visit a sick parishioner. The piano keys jumped alive with the syncopated rhythm of ragtime, the notes bouncing enticingly about with a wink and a grin.

Side by side with Anna, Nessie held their clasped hands up between them. "First we hold our head and shoulders like this, kinda elegant-like. Then walk with fast little steps around like this." They wound a path around the other dancers and back to the edge of the tent. "Now, the fun part. Watch Little John over there."

They watched him lean back, smooth and lanky, and prance like a high-stepping thoroughbred, and synchronize quick little heel-toe slides with his pretty dance partner.

In short time, Anna and Nessie were laughing and prancing, maneuvering skillfully around the other cakewalkers. The nods and smiles under that tent said one thing, that there was nothing more important and nothing more joyful than this moment.

Nessie's heart was so full that she felt it would explode in her chest. Lewis was happy and safe, and she had Anna's hand warm and firmly in her own. And when Anna turned with a smile just for her, Nessie knew that the world right at that moment was perfect and right. She could think of no reason that it wouldn't always be.

"Will they play another like that?" Anna asked. "That was so much fun. Let's dance another."

The requests for more ragtime made it clear that Nessie and Anna weren't the only ones who wanted to keep dancing, and the musicians happily accommodated. They played piece after piece, notes bouncing irreverently, ragged and alive, until only young legs were able to continue.

When the music slowed and Nessie and Anna caught their breath, a young man approached them. He placed his palm across his chest and nodded first to Anna, and then to Nessie. "Rufus Tinker," he said. "Your momma give her permission to this fine dancer to ask your fine self to dance this next one. So, I'm askin', Miss Nessie."

He was as tall as Lewis, and thin as a willow whip, with a smile that could turn a mother's ire into an extra piece of pecan pie. He'd caught her thoughts off guard, reveling in the closeness with Anna, who had no worries of the boys asking her to dance. She hadn't willed it, hadn't seen it coming, but there seemed to be no way to avoid it. This dance was to be Rufus Tinker's.

It had been close to perfect, today—experiencing this special day with Lewis, and sharing it with Anna. It had allowed Nessie's mind to go beyond, into what if, into a future of special hope. Her and Anna's future. Their adventure, going off to school, making changes, making a difference. The money from doing laundry and ironing, the extra jobs for the ladies at Anna's church, which even Momma didn't know about, would see to it. It was safely stashed away in a jar under the floor of their little house, growing with possibility day by day.

Nessie was only half listening to Rufus's story of how he and her cousin, Jimmy, had deposited a huge pile of fresh horse manure right behind the outhouse and had pulled the nails from the boards behind the seat. They hadn't waited long, hiding behind a water trough, before Rufus's uncle sat back, fell through the boards, and landed bare-assed into the pile of manure.

Yes, she remembered hearing the stories of silliness. She had wondered then, as she wondered now, how boys could be so accomplished at times, and yet so completely childlike at others.

She smiled nonetheless.

"Can't think of a better gift Miss Grayson could give Lewis and his bride," Rufus continued. "She's a generous woman."

"Anna says that her grandmother loves seeing everyone havin' such a good time."

"It's one of the best times I seen, cuz for me, I got to dance with the prettiest girl in this whole county."

Nessie diverted her eyes past his left shoulder. "I say you sure haven't met many girls, then, Rufus Tinker."

He'd caught her off guard again, made her believe for a moment that he meant what he said. So it didn't matter how many girls he had met, or how many he had danced with, he thought she was special. And for that moment, so did Nessie.

"Aw, you jes' want me to tell you why I think you're so pretty," he said, as the musicians put their dance to rest. "Shall I tell you?"

She swore his smile was sweet with mischief. It tempted her for only a second. "You go on, now," she said, "tell your nonsense to another girl.

I thank you for that fine dance, though." Nessie offered a quick smile, then turned away.

"It ain't nonsense I'm telling," he replied, watching her slip around couples headed for refreshments. "You'll see."

Silliness. That was the best that could be said for time wasted on the likes of boys. Nessie garnished the thought with a fresh dash of gratefulness as she burst through the door of their little house to find Anna waiting.

"I thought for sure that you would beat me here, Ness. I took extra time to be sure that Gram has everything she needs for the night. Her hips are painin' her so today . . . I wish we didn't have to be back by dark, though."

"I hurried the best I could, but every time I gathered up a load of dishes, that Rufus was there claimin' to help me carry 'em. He did more talkin' and walkin' backwards than he did carryin'. I'd been done long ago without his help."

Nessie plopped down on the cot next to Anna and fished the coins from her apron pocket.

"He's sweet on you, Ness."

"Well, I give him no reason to be. No silly boy can do what this is gonna do." She counted out her money, jumped up and retrieved her jar from under the loose floorboard. "It's a good thing I had to go change clothes after the party. I was so excited about the wedding that I left the money in my apron right there on the kitchen chair."

"When are you finally going to tell your momma what you're savin' for?"

"I can't tell her I'm savin' at all. She thinks like my grandma more than not. They don't see no need for me to have money of my own. The family'll take care of me 'til I get married. All she'll be talkin' 'bout tonight is me and that Rufus."

"I'm glad my Gram knows. Look, I finished another." Anna picked up a raven-haired doll with a long black shirt and white blouse, and handed it to Nessie.

Tiny stitches fashioned the features of the doll's face and formed the hands and fingers of fine linen. Nessie fingered the delicate sleeves of the miniature blouse. "It's beautiful, Anna. Who's buying this one?"

"Mr. Langford at the Post Office. His wife saw the one I made for Mrs. Jenkins' daughter, and she wanted one for her daughter. I finished in good time for her birthday."

Nessie smiled. "All of Atlanta's gonna want one of your special dolls. And I got more people wantin' to give me work than I can fit in a week."

"It's grand, Ness. Our own money, earned and deserved. Yes, indeed." She wrinkled her nose as she always did just before flashing a smile as grand as her plans.

"And no one to tell us what we have to do with it. It's grand all right. And Miss Tilton's been tellin' me all about Spelman College. She's been talkin' to me about where I might be able to room, and everything."

"Are we going to be able to see each other every day? Where is the rooming house?"

"There's a place called Neighborhood House," Nessie replied. "The church helps support it so that people like me can afford to stay there and go to school. But Miss Tilton said that it's not far from Spelman, and that means it's in the Negro section. Everything is so separate, no mixed neighborhoods or business sections anymore. It wouldn't be good for you to take the trolley there."

"Let's see when we go to town. Maybe if I can find a place close. If I can't go to your room, maybe you could come to mine. We could still share special books that we find, and tell each other all about our day and what we learned."

"I'll drive your grandma's buggy, and we can go all over and look for the perfect place. We have to find one."

"If we do, you'll have to tell them."

Nessie took a long breath and let it out slowly. Then with a nod, she said, "I know."

"Who do you worry about telling most, your momma or your papa?"

"Momma," she said without hesitation. "Papa would hear me out. He's always given me more room than the boys. He set the boundaries for them, and sort of left my boundaries to Momma."

"Will she be mad?"

"No. She just won't hear of it."

16

Anna neatly wrapped the Langford doll in tissue paper and tucked it in one of the boxes Mr. Barker at the mercantile saved for her. Saturday was going to be a busy day, and she wanted everything ready tonight so that she and Nessie could get an early start in the morning.

Downstairs, the music from the phonograph had gone silent, and Addy, her knitting resting unattended on her lap, had fallen asleep on the love seat. A voice calling Anna's name—authoritative, masculine, and barely holding the edge of civility—woke Addy.

She rose, her hips stiff and defiant, and moved slowly into the hall as Thomas called again. "Anna."

"I'm coming, Papa." Anna's hurried steps creaked along the upstairs hallway.

"What is it, Thomas?" Addy asked. "Is there something wrong?"

"I'll speak with Anna," he replied, his eyes focused on the top of the stairs.

Her steps slowed, but Anna's heart rate increased at the sight of her father and her grandmother in what she had come to recognize as a standoff. She'd seen many of them over the years—cheeks twitching with words red hot to be said and unrelenting stares. Barely managed restraint, and thinly disguised animosity would be closed behind the library door, and the rest was always left to Anna's imagination. But during the past couple of years, after her father had moved to the apartment above his office, their frequency had lessened. This one, she feared, wouldn't make it to the library.

"You need to tell me what this is about," Addy insisted.

"Proper conduct for a young woman, Adeline. Something that you have never seemed to grasp." He set a stern eye on Anna, now near the bottom of the stairs. "I'll speak with my daughter alone."

"You will not."

"What is it, Papa?"

He seemed undecided, weighing his options. Addy remained unmoved by his glare. He turned a less harsh version toward Anna.

"I thought you made the dolls for the church, for their charity drive, Anna."

"I did. Everyone loved them, Papa." Her hope lifted for that rare positive talk, for something complimentary. Just a little hope that the strained air between her father and grandmother, this time, would not include her. Just a little.

"People are saying that you are selling them."

"For a fair price," she replied. "And they are genuinely glad to pay it. They've even said so."

His focus turned sharply to Addy. "How do you allow this, Adeline? You know how this looks. Do you take no pride in this family's good name?"

"Pride, Thomas?" Addy held a hard stare, offered nary a blink. "Is that what brings you out here for a few hours on Sundays? Is it pride that allows you to find out what is happening in your daughter's lives from town folk? Have they told you yet that Emily claims to be spending time with you when she is actually seeing a boy who works at the hardware store?"

"I have forbidden her from seeing him. It's been taken care of."

"Might the fact that she has been lying to both of us be of more importance than Anna making her own money?"

They went on as if Anna were not standing within an outstretched arm of them, as if she held no stake in their banter's outcome.

"Unlike Anna," Thomas continued, "Emily knows what I expect of her. She understands the proper behavior for a young woman of her age. And until they are married, my daughters are my responsibility. I have made sure that they have what they need. Anything more, they know that they only have to come to me for it."

"Haven't you noticed that long ago they decided that having to explain to you why they wanted your permission for this or that, was no longer worth the effort?"

His attention changed immediately to Anna. "I won't have you pandering wares like a pauper. What is it you want the money for?"

She hadn't expected to have to answer that question today. She had, in fact, planned to avoid it altogether. He hadn't told her anything that she didn't already know. What was expected of her had been clear for as long as she could remember. It was possibility that she had found on her own. It was possibility that allowed her to answer him.

"I'm going to go to nursing school."

"No, Anna," he said, shaking his head. "There is no purpose in that. You are a fine-looking young woman, with all the domestic skills necessary. Your mother, and your grandmother saw to that quite well. There is no reason that you won't marry, and marry well."

"But I may *choose* not to marry. And I choose to have a career where I can make a difference, where I can make things better for others."

He shook his head again. "That is for women of lower means, with few choices in life. Not for you or your sister."

"Are you forbidding me, Papa, as you forbade Emily? Forbidding me to—"

But her grandmother's hand, quickly placed on Anna's arm, drew the line that stopped her.

"You've made your point clear, Thomas. There is no need for further discussion. I understand your concern," Addy said, releasing Anna's arm, "and I truly appreciate your talks with Emily, since she tends to avoid talking with me."

"Well, Adeline, that's my responsibility, and I do take that seriously."

Addy's hand appeared again on Anna's arm, a reminder for silence.

"And I will expect in the future," he continued, "when I give a young man my permission to court you, that it will not be met with resistance."

Anna understood the gentle squeeze of her arm. "Yes, sir," she replied.

"Good, good," he said. "Now, if there is anything you need, either of you, you come and talk to me. I've already reminded Emily."

"Thank you, Thomas," Addy said with a final release of Anna's arm. "I do appreciate that."

He nodded, straightened his shoulders, and tugged at the bottom of his vest. One more nod, and he turned and left.

At the sound of the closing door, Anna spoke first. "He's forbidding me, Gram."

"Come," Addy said, turning stiffly. "We'll talk about it."

Addy settled with a groan in her favorite spot on the love seat, and motioned for Anna to join her.

"Why doesn't it matter what I want to do?" Anna asked as she sat next to her grandmother.

"It matters, Anna. It matters to me."

"But you hushed me as though—"

"Because you must learn when to speak your thoughts, and when to make other use of them. It's a lesson I learned a very long time ago, and learning it has served me well."

"I'll not change Papa's mind, will I?"

"It's unlikely, and the energy you waste in trying can be better used to find your own way."

"Without his permission?"

"With my permission. Though I dare say even that isn't needed. You are a smart young woman, with goodness in your heart. What's important is for you to find what makes you happy in this life. Maybe that will be going to school and learning how you can help others, and maybe you will marry."

"I don't think my life would be happy if I married. I never want to be as unhappy as Momma was."

"Then don't let anyone decide for you, Anna. Marry only if you find someone who sees your needs and wishes equal to their own. It must be someone who knows your heart and someone who you will want to spend the rest of your days and nights with."

"Is that how you felt about the Captain?"

There was a longer than thoughtful hesitation. Addy's eyes left Anna's to focus somewhere across the room. Anna waited patiently until the pale blue eyes returned.

"There are times," she began, "when it seems that was a part of someone else's life, the time with the Captain." She dropped her gaze and smoothed a nonexistent wrinkle from her dress. "No," she continued, "I didn't feel those things that I want for you, for the Captain."

"But you married him."

Addy nodded. "I didn't know that I didn't have to. By everyone else's account he was the perfect husband for me. He was strong of conviction and confident. By most standards, I dare say that he was respected and successful. I was young, Anna, not much older than you. I had no idea of love."

"Did you ever find it? Love, I mean."

"Just for a moment, such a brief moment."

"When?" There was a spike of excitement in Anna's voice. "Who was he? What happened?"

"Too long ago," Addy replied, her focus wandering again. "Sometimes, late at night, I think that it wasn't long enough ago." Her eyes, painfully serious, returned to Anna's. "I'm sure that Billy's love was more than I deserved. But, I've never wanted another love more."

"Billy?" The excitement of a secret being revealed was uncontainable. "The Billy doll. Grandma, is it the same Billy?"

"The same Billy," she said. "I made that doll for your mother when she was a child. I'm not sure why."

"What happened to Billy?"

"He was killed." Addy's brow pressed into a deep crease above her nose. "But, we won't talk of that now."

"Was he killed in the war, like the Captain?"

"Another time, Anna," she said with the tone of finality that Anna knew not to challenge. "There will be another time. What's important now is you. You must not let anyone else set limits on what you can achieve. No one else knows what is in your heart, and no one but God knows your limits." Addy reached over and patted Anna's hand. "Now go on and get Mr. Langford's doll ready."

So much to absorb, so much to think about—advice, solid and unquestionable. But as Anna hurried back to her room, the thought that quickened her steps was telling Nessie about Billy. It had been their curiosity since childhood, and it was unraveling, and right now that was all she could think about.

17

Nessie had managed to contain her excitement long enough to walk nearly the entire path to Anna's. It was a big day, and she was freshly bathed and dressed in her best skirt and blouse. But as soon as she saw Anna putting her things in the buggy, she gathered her skirt and burst into a run.

"Anna," she called out in the last breathless yards. "Oh, Anna, I can't stand it any longer."

"I know," Anna replied. "This is going to be a wonderful day."

"No, so much more. I couldn't sleep last night at all. I wanted to come tell you what I found out."

"What?" Anna grasped Nessie's hands. "Tell me then, Ness. What is it?"

"Yes, but not here." Nessie released Anna's hands and scrambled into the buggy. "Hurry," she said. "I'll tell you on the way so no one can hear."

A good way down the drive, but before the main road, Anna could wait no longer. She grasped Nessie's arm. "Here, Ness, stop here. You must tell me. What is it?"

Nessie brought the buggy to a stop, and turned to Anna's anxious expression. "I didn't expect it," Nessie began. "I was just tellin' Momma what your grandma told you about love and Billy, and she got this look on her face, a strange look I've never seen before, and she said, 'You listen to me. You must never tell anyone, you hear?'"

"About Billy? I don't—"

"I didn't understand, either. And Momma must have thought I knew a lot more than I did. She said that the secret's been kept all these years, and that the Captain's death was a blessing for everyone.

And, *then*, she said that my grandpa never told anyone where he buried the Captain."

Anna's expression looked like she couldn't decide whether to ask why, or when, or how, so Nessie kept going. "I was afraid to ask anything for fear Momma would figure out that I didn't know at all what she was talkin' about. So, I just told her that I would never give up secrets, especially about our family. Well, that's when the part that makes believin' hard, came out." Nessie stopped for a breath.

"What, Nessie? *What?*"

"She said, not just for our family, but for yours, too, the secret's got to be kept. You got to promise, too, Anna."

"Of course. Of course. You know you never have to ask that. Now, tell me."

"Momma said that most would only see the Captain's chivalry, comin' home from the battle close by, and seein' Billy standin' there under the big tree with your grandma. She said grandpa never would say if Billy was wearin' a Union jacket. But, most would put no blame for him killin' Billy right there."

"No," Anna exclaimed. "No, no. Gram saw it?"

"But that's not the worst of it, Anna. Your grandmother grabbed the rifle she kept there for marauders, and shot the Captain dead herself."

The look of shock and disbelief on Anna's face was the same expression Nessie had worked so hard to keep from showing her mother. But as hard as the image was to envision, she must have somehow managed to mask the shock.

"I don't know what is harder to hear—that your grandma loved someone else, or that she killed the Captain."

"You should have seen her eyes, Ness, when she told me about Billy. I've never seen anything like it. It was like she could still see him, like he was standing there across the room, and she was saying one more time how much she loved him. That somehow he would know that again."

Nessie's voice was a whisper. "Oh, Anna."

"There was nothing I could say. And now knowing that she saw Billy killed, I just want to cry."

Nessie nodded. "I'm sorry I told you somethin' so sad."

"No, it's okay, Nessie. There seems to be so much that you and I don't know about our families, about how much they have been a part of each other's lives for so long."

"We're grown enough now, I expect."

"Are we?" Anna asked. "Sometimes I don't want to think about anything but how many fish we'll catch."

"Me, too. But then I get somethin' naggin' at me to know more about not just what things happened in the past, but why. Don't you wonder that? Don't you wonder why?"

"I do," Anna said. "But, not today. I want to spend today planning our tomorrows."

"Then that's what we'll do," Nessie said with a snap of the reins.

The city was a bustle of activity. Buggies and wagons filled the streets and trolley cars were full. Small groups, gathered in conversation, dotted the walks while others hurried along to shops and theaters and restaurants.

The girls went straight to the post office first, where Anna delivered Mr. Langford's doll and Nessie waited with the buggy.

It was glorious, Nessie thought, a day that was all theirs, a day to test their plan and peek into their future. Nessie touched the head of her hatpin, making sure that it was secure, and smiled to no one in particular. It was just that kind of feeling.

A moment later, Anna, sporting her brightest smile, climbed into the buggy. "Look," she said excitedly, "he gave me more than I asked. He said it was the finest present he could give his daughter and he gave me a dollar and fifty cents."

It was wonderful news, right up there high on the list that made today so good. "And you can be sure that his daughter is gonna to show her friends," Nessie said, "and before long you're gonna have more orders than you ever imagined, and more money, too."

"It's exciting to be sure," Anna replied. "I'll have to stitch every night to keep up." She rolled her eyes. "And that means Emily will make sure Papa knows how much I'm embarrassing the family."

"Maybe you could bribe her."

"That's an enticing idea," she replied with a grin. "But," her words seemed to bounce, "I'm not going to let her ruin our day. Let's go to the mercantile and I'll buy us licorice sticks to celebrate."

Nessie moved the buggy down the block and parked around the corner closest to the store. Anna sprang from the buggy, her braid bobbing against her back as she hurried to make her purchase. Moments later they were savoring their treats and giggling at the silliest notions. They entertained bribery ideas, fun diversions that lacked possibility, until they were interrupted by a family approaching and crossing the street in front of the buggy. Nessie fell silent immediately and lowered her head. The next second, Anna stopped mid-giggle, nodded as the woman looked her way, and offered her best after-church smile.

Her smile lasted only until the family's attention turned to admiring the new buildings, built to replace whole blocks destroyed by the big fire. The girls waited quietly until the family had moved slowly down the street and around the corner.

"Come on, Nessie, let's go look at a boarding house near the nursing school."

It hadn't been a conscious thought until now, at least Nessie hadn't held it long enough to feel its impact. But now, as they traveled the streets in this section of town, it seemed that they were a whole world away from Spelman and the Negro housing that Miss Tilton had told her about. Block by block, the sense of change, of how different life was about to become, surrounded her in real tangible form and she was forced to face it. In less than two months, Anna would be here and for the first time in Nessie's life, she could no longer count on seeing her every day. Weekends, Anna had promised, and each day after classes, they would spend together—sharing the events of the day, studying together. It was unfathomable to imagine that it couldn't be, that she would not know when she would see Anna's smile or hear her laugh.

Nessie stopped the buggy in front of a fine old house, and tried shutting the unbearable from her thoughts.

"I wish you could come in with me, Nessie, and tell me what you think. You might sense things that I don't."

"You can tell me everything after. Write everything down in your mind, and ask lots of questions."

Anna jumped from the buggy, and straightened the band of her skirt. "Well, then," she said, "here I go."

It was a large old Georgian with a wide front porch, an immaculately manicured front yard and a brick walk leading directly from the street to the front steps. Anna turned once to look at Nessie, then knocked on the door. A matronly woman greeted her, looked past her to the buggy, and invited her in.

"I'll be attending nursing school," Anna explained, "and I'm looking into places to stay nearby."

"Well, this is as fine a place as you will find," the woman said. "Come. Let me show you around."

The tour began in the parlor, where the woman laid out the rules of no gentlemen visitors past 8:00—and never above the first floor. It continued through the dining area with scheduled mealtimes, to the sleeping room upstairs. With practiced efficiency, the woman showed her the bathroom and laundry facilities, and explained the accompanying expectations of chores. Simple furnishings, immaculately kept. All needs met. And with such a thorough presentation, there had been no need for questions. None, at least, that came to mind.

Back downstairs, the woman ushered Anna through the kitchen to a door at the back of the house, and continued. "The building there," she pointed through the screen door, "is where your Negro will stay."

"Oh, but—"

"You won't have need to go out there. There is a bell system, the bell that I pointed out in your room, and should you need your Negro at any time, you just ring and she will come to this door."

Anna turned to look toward the front of the house as if she could see Nessie waiting in the buggy. "But," she readdressed the woman, "she's not . . . she won't be . . ."

"Well, if you change your mind—"

"I . . . no . . . I'm sorry. I need to go now."

She left the house without her normal courtesies, scurried down the front walk to the buggy, and avoided eye contact with Nessie.

"What?" Nessie said, leaning toward Anna. "What is it?"

Anna shook her head, straightened her skirt beneath her, and said nothing.

"Did you not like it? Is it too expensive?"

"Let's go home."

"We'll find another, Anna, one that you like." But even as she said the words, she sensed something much more wrong than the dislike of a boarding house. Something was desperately wrong. Anna's eyes remained down and Nessie leaned forward to see if there were tears. She reached for Anna's arm, aware of nothing beyond Anna being upset, and when she turned away, Nessie leaned closer.

In the next instant, a hand grabbed Nessie's arm and yanked her from the buggy with such force that it sent her sprawling to the ground.

A man, about the age of her father, leaned over the seat toward a surprised Anna. "Are you all right, Miss?"

"Fine," she replied. "I'm fine, just not feeling well." She glanced quickly at Nessie retrieving her hat from the ground.

"I'll get my buggy," he said, "and see that you get home safely."

"Oh, no, there's no need." Anna spoke as Nessie stood silently, her arms at her side, her focus on the ground. "Nessie," she said sharply, "get up here, and drive me home this minute."

"Yes, ma'am," Nessie replied. She waited for the man to step aside.

He moved only after a warning. "You mind your place, Negro. And see to it that your mistress gets home safely."

"Yes, sir," Nessie replied. She climbed into the buggy, her focus directed over the horse's back and avoiding even so much as a glance toward Anna.

"Now," Anna directed, before Nessie could even get the reins in hand. A "ha" from Nessie and a flick of the reins, and the buggy lunged forward into the street.

There had never been a time, in all of their growing up years, when there was a silence like this between them. There was always something needing to be shared, and things needing sorting and supporting. Nothing was ever too important, or too scary, or too personal. They shared their fears and wonders. They laughed and promised and wished. And now, silence.

Even well past the eyes and ears of the busy city, alone on the road and clear of judgment, there was only the steady clomping of the horse's hooves and the creaking of the buggy.

The thoughts came easier than Nessie wanted, assuaged by the gentle sway of the horse's caramel-colored tail. She'd fought their emergence all during the day, pushing them away each time with the brightness of the day or a promise of a long held hope. But they came easier now, washing through her consciousness as the tears began streaking down her cheeks.

She should banish them, those hope-killing thoughts, render them powerless, face them down with the certainty that they were wrong. But the truth was, she was no longer certain that they were. She wasn't even sure that Anna still clung to the same possibilities, the same hopes. What did seem certain, sadly certain today, was that there were things that wishes could not change, and places where dreams could never be more than dreams. And tears, her own or Anna's, could do nothing but confirm it.

The buggy had barely come to a stop in front of the barn. Anna jumped to the ground, and without a word or a glance, began running toward the path. For the next few moments, Nessie sat stunned, reins still in her hands, unsure of what to do. Leave her be, to sort, to struggle alone? Or follow and do what they had always done, face whatever it was together?

Nessie jumped from the buggy and ran to the path. It was the right thing, the only thing. She needed to be with Anna.

Ahead, Anna raced to the door without looking back once. Nessie, clutching her hat in her hand, closed the distance to their place as fast as she could run.

Breathless, Nessie burst through the door to find Anna lying face down on the cot, crying. "Oh, Anna," Nessie said, "tell me. Please tell me."

Anna rolled to her side, reached for Nessie's hand, and pulled her down to lie next to her. "It's all wrong, Ness." Anna held Nessie tightly to her, pressing her face into Nessie's shoulder. "It's all so terribly wrong."

There were a lot of things that were wrong, of course there were. Nessie could list them, the ones needing to be changed, those that she was pretty sure would never change. Yes, she could name them, possibly even guess which one was making Anna cry, but right now she wanted only to close her eyes and feel Anna's arms around her. For as long as she could, she wanted to breathe in the scent of her hair, the sweet oils from the heat of her neck, and to feel her breath, calming now, warm against her face. Warmth took over Nessie's body, radiating from their embrace and highlighting every inch of her touching Anna's body.

"You should hate me, Ness." Anna spoke softly, her forehead pressed against Nessie's cheek. "You would be right to."

Nessie ran her hand over the top of Anna's head, over the smooth silky hair, once, and then again. "No, I could never."

"*I* hate me," Anna said, lifting her head to look at Nessie. "How can *you* not?"

"Why do you say that?" Nessie relaxed her head back onto her grandmother's old feather pillow.

Anna shifted to lean over her, a confession, nearly nose to nose. "Because I let it be, like it was all right." Anna's brow knit into a tight crease above her nose. "I let that woman at the boarding house talk about you like you were no more than a pack mule, and that man . . ." She carefully touched her fingers to the flawless brown skin of Nessie's cheek. "Nessie, I let him hurt you."

She felt her skin flush with heat where Anna touched her, so aware of the length of Anna's body pressed against her side. "No," Nessie replied, "You didn't let him. It's the way it is, that's all." Anna lifted her head slightly, concern still deeply set in the blue of her eyes. "I can take a tumble better than most," Nessie continued, "growin' up with all them boys."

"It's not just the tumble," Anna said as she pushed herself up and leaned back against the darkened wood boards between the studs. "It's all of it, how they think about you and how they treat you, and how they expect me to do the same. I didn't tell them that they were wrong to do that. I didn't tell them that I would never think the way they do . . . I let it be."

"Papa would say that you did right. Lettin' it be keeps us both safe. He raised us up to know who we are. Other people not knowin' won't change that."

"How did they do it, the women we read about? How did they make things different? I wish we could talk to them. You know, ask them right out."

"I'd ask 'em if they were scared." Nessie pushed herself up to rest on her elbow. "And what made 'em so brave."

"I don't think I can be that brave." Anna ran her hand along Nessie's arm to her hand, and grasped it. "And I don't want to be any place where I can't see you every day."

Anna had put it in words, said out loud the very thing that Nessie had hoped and wondered, and even claimed as true without the words ever being said. And now, there it was, said out loud and sealed with knowing that there was no one Nessie could trust with bare honesty more than her.

Hearing it said did not change what Nessie knew was inevitable, what even truth couldn't change, but it allowed her to set it aside, for now. Maybe for a long time.

It was enough to make her smile, to make her sit up and nestle into Anna's embrace. "I would hate any day that I couldn't see you," she said, as Anna tightened her arms and rested her cheek against Nessie's head.

"Then, we'll stay here in our little house. That's what we'll do."

18

It became the summer of denial. Neither Nessie nor Anna spoke of it—what they were denying, or how long they thought they could. They spoke with no reference past the next day—today this, tomorrow that—because neither of them wanted to see what was beyond. Maybe the days of seeing each other every day were numbered, but Nessie would not be counting. She chose, instead, to believe the lilt in Anna's voice, and let it lift her past the truth. Even while what she knew clung stubbornly to the hem of her denial, Nessie reveled in Anna's smile and lost herself in the blue of her eyes. For now, they were hers.

The threat of rain had passed, and the humidity tempered by the afternoon sun burst to brilliance between passing clouds. One line of laundry already hung, Nessie worked on pinning up the second line. She shook a pillowcase straight with a snap, sending a fresh scent of Borax into the air, and pinned it to the line with a wooden pin.

As she stretched to place the second pin in place, the hung laundry behind her separated and arms wrapped around Nessie's waist. "Save me, Ness," Anna said against the side of her face. "Save me."

Nessie dropped her arms to cover Anna's and giggled at the tight embrace. "Another one?" she asked, as Anna kissed the side of her face and released her.

"Gerald Baxter," Anna replied.

Nessie turned to see Anna roll her eyes. "Your Papa's just gonna keep sendin' suitors, you know."

"Well, starting today there will be no one there to suit. I'm not going to do it—sit there all prim and proper and make boring talk with a boring boy. And Emily—I don't want to hear another word from her—don't muss your hair, don't talk too much, be agreeable. Yeah, well, I'd rather speak my mind, and smell like outdoor air and garden soil."

"Me, too. Come on," Nessie said, grabbing a shirt from the laundry basket, "help me hang the rest of this."

Anna scooped a handful of clothespins from the bag hanging on the line. "We have to hurry, and then disappear. Gram will send Emily looking for me."

With the last shirt hastily hung, the girls ducked under the lines and behind Nessie's house, around the barn, and rushed along the edge of the field toward the creek. Emily would go as far as Nessie's house, and that would be the extent of her search. No one was going to look for Anna at the fishing spot.

Through the years it had remained as Nessie remembered it the first time Lewis brought her fishing with him. The changes subtle and easily unnoticed, were nature's own—smaller branches, weathered and gone, new ones taking their place, and water level rising and falling with each year's rainfall. This year the water was high on the banks, the special pool formed by the fallen tree trunk, full and deep.

Breathless from their escape run, the girls slowed their pace to a walk through the high grass above the bank. At their spot, they pulled up the back hem of their skirts and tucked them into their waistbands, and quickly shed their socks and shoes.

"This is my second favorite spot in the whole world," Nessie said, lowering herself onto the log and dropping her legs into the cool water.

Anna sat and inched her way out on the log beside Nessie. "We've not seen much of that whole world, Ness, but I bet if we had, this would surely stay a favorite."

Nessie focused on the slow circular movements she made with her feet in the water. Fresh, cool currents washed around her legs. "Do you think we'll see any of the world?"

"I don't think I want to if it's anything like what we see in town." Anna hooked her foot behind Nessie's ankle and lifted it up to the surface and back down. "There's no place where we could stay together, not here. We'd have to move North. Gram said that a lot of people have."

"Does she know someone who left? We could write to them, ask them how much money we would need, and where we could stay."

"Maybe she does, Ness."

Nessie saw it, right that moment in Anna's eyes, the same hope that was swelling its possibilities in herself. Oh, how much she wanted to believe it. Could there really be a way, a future past the summer? A future with Anna?

"What about nursing school? Anna, you gotta go to school."

"There must be one in the North. And a school for you, too. We don't have to go right away. We'll have to save more money, and write letters."

"I'll ask Miss Tilton, too, who we should write to." Nessie covered Anna's hand on the log between them, and met her eyes. "Can we really do this?"

"Sure we can. You want to, don't you?"

"More than anything," Nessie replied. "But what if we get there and it's just like here. And we spent our money and left our families, and it's not like we hoped?"

"We'll be all right, Ness. As long as we have each other. If we have to, we can come back and stay right here again."

"Come on," Nessie said, "let's go count how much money we have so far."

19

Thomas's tone charged the line of civility. "I won't allow it, Adeline."
He paced, heavy steps in front of Addy, who sat rigidly on the edge
of the love seat. "Such an ill-conceived decision." He turned with a
forceful wave of his hand to face her. "Irresponsible, Adeline."

Addy watched him, refusing to lower her eyes from the force of
his words. She had faced worse, so much worse. Thomas's held no
weight to a Sherman lieutenant with fire at his back and the cause at
the front. His anger allowed him only to ignore the impotency of his
power, to believe that he had control over her.

"And, what would you do, Thomas? Wait for the weevil to wipe us
out? It's only a matter of time. If not the agriculture reports, what
then would you base your decision on, a sense that it couldn't happen
to you? Or, is it that it's my decision, because you are not in a position
to allow it, or not?"

"You know nothing about raising livestock. Your foreman knows
nothing of it, or your workers. You have to build fences and a barn,
and invest capital in start-up stock and feed. You don't understand
the cost, or the risk."

"There is risk either way. By cutting the cotton crop in half, and
adding livestock, we take the lesser of those risks. We educate ourselves,
and we phase out cotton on our own terms, not at the mercy of an
insect." She watched him turn his back. "I don't want to argue with
you, Thomas. I thought that by explaining my decision I could put
your mind at ease, so that you don't worry needlessly about the girls."

"The girls," he nearly shouted as he turned, "will be fine once they
are married. That is, unless you have filled them so full of nonsensical
notions that you have spoiled them for the likes of a good man."

"Spoiled?" She replied with the stern look of a challenge. "You surely don't mean that they would be too confident in their own minds, or secure in their own decisions. Would there be no man capable of respecting those attributes?"

"Your widowhood has not served you well, I'm afraid. I should have seen that earlier. I should have taken another wife to see to the girls' proper upbringing. But, my love for your Mary has never allowed for it."

"Well, then," Addy replied, "I say you ought to blame that on me as well."

"He's going to do it," Nessie said, the moment Anna appeared at the back door. "Papa told us today. He met with your grandma and Mr. Shakly, and they all decided it was best."

"That's why I gotta get outta here, Ness." Anna let the screen door swing loose behind her and cleared the steps with two bounds. "Let's go."

They started out at a run, and once they were deep into the path, they settled into a brisk walk.

"Gram was explaining why she made the decision, and now it's a full-out argument. Papa's furious."

"What's he so mad about? Everybody's been sayin' we've been lucky so far—burnin' the fields down at the end of the season to keep the weevil at bay."

"Gram told him that, told him what the agriculture reports say about what will happen if we get infested, or a farm nearby. But, he's got no say in it, and that makes him mad. Can't leave that kind of decision-making up to a woman and a foreman."

"Mr. Shakly knows a lot. Papa says he reads up on all the reports, and he shares what he learns with Papa even though it's your grandma who pays him."

"Gram trusts him, and he treats her with the same respect that he would give a man that he worked for."

"Papa must really trust him. He'd never take a chance like this if he didn't. Cuttin' down the cotton crop means cutting the acres that they rent out to other farmers, too. I overheard Papa talkin' to Grandpa about what to do if it doesn't work and they lose money."

"What would they do?" Anna asked.

"Papa said he could try to get a loan, but Grandpa wouldn't hear of it. He said if they couldn't make a payment the bank could take the land. I don't want to think about what that would mean."

They reached the clearing by the creek and followed it along the bank. It was always so peaceful here, the gurgle of water navigating the rocks at the bend, and intermittent plops as turtles left their sunbathing posts on the half-submerged logs. Peaceful. Mother Nature in no hurry. The slowness of the sun, the only marker of time.

"I think Papa is scared," Nessie began. "I know Grandpa is. I heard him say how he don't know livestock like he knows cotton."

"Gram doesn't sound worried. She never does. It seems like cutting back and risking only half a crop is a smart plan. Of course, if the crop and the livestock fail . . ."

"Are you worried?" Nessie asked.

Anna pushed aside bent-over brush with the toe of her shoe—slow pace, slow to answer. "Gram would never accept help from Papa. I'm sure of it. She would be afraid that it would give him rights to her property. I think she would sell it before she did that."

"My grandfather expects everyone in the family to do everything they can to keep our land. It's very important to him, and to Papa. He won't ask, he won't have to."

"I would do that for Gram," Anna said. "If I don't go to school, that would mean I could be here if she needs me. I could keep making dolls."

Nessie knew that about Anna. She knew a lot of things about her that had never been put into words. Like knowing that what her grandmother did meant more to Anna than anything her Papa said. Anna would never have to tell her that—or that fairness is a practice, and love is an action. Things you don't save up for special, but do everyday. Reasons as concrete as they come for loving her.

"But, what if you go to school, Anna, and become a nurse like you want. You could work at the hospital and earn more money than the dolls make. Then, if she needed help . . ."

Anna stopped her toe-pushing amble and looked up. She didn't make eye contact, but looked across the creek—an expressionless stare that had become far more frequent this summer. Sometimes it lasted so long that Nessie began to think she wouldn't tell her what she was thinking. But Nessie had learned that if she waited, didn't push her past her thoughts, then Anna would finally tell her.

"I worry about her," Anna said, bringing her focus back to Nessie's eyes. "She's slowed down a lot. The women come to meet at the house now, so that she doesn't have to make the trip to town."

"My momma's there everyday. It's not part of her pay, but you know she watches out for your grandma like she's family."

"I know, Ness. I've counted on your momma more than I did my own. But I can't count on Emily. She spends a lot of time in town. There might be no one in the house with her."

Anna took Nessie's hand and pulled her to a small clearing near their fishing spot, where the weeds were tamped down like a grass mat. She settled cross-legged on the ground, and Nessie sat next to her, hugging her knees.

"It isn't my decision alone, it's our decision together, Ness. If I stay, then what happens to our plan? Nobody's going to let us stay together, and I won't treat you like they want. I love you too much to do that."

It began in Anna's eyes, the movement, glimmering in blue, and brought the softness of her lips to touch so lightly on Nessie's. There was that second, the wonder, what it meant, where it might go, and then—the gentle warmth caused her eyes to close as Anna's lips pressed full against her own. It needed no permission—the kiss, the feeling—only acceptance.

Her lips softened, accepted. She didn't wonder, didn't question or really think at all. The moment was too centered, too perfect. She was closer to Anna than she had ever been to anyone. Closer than a whisper, closer than a secret.

Nessie slid her arm around Anna, and pressed her lips into the warmth of her first kiss. She had imagined it, her first time, with

117

Rufus, just once. But this, melting her lips into Anna's, oh yes, she'd imagined it many times. The imagining of it, though, had never come close to this, never hinted at the heat that it started. She wanted it to continue, to take the breath from her, to be the only, the all, the world standing still. She wanted nothing more at that moment, only Anna, pressing against her with no tomorrow.

But, of course, there would be a tomorrow, and the seconds after Anna pulled her lips away and touched them to Nessie's neck. A time finally for words. The words, a whisper against Nessie's ear. "It's all right, isn't it?" Nessie nodded, and pressed the side of her face to Anna's.

"I wanted it to be all right," Anna said, moving to look into Nessie's eyes.

"Did you ever want to do that before?" Nessie asked.

Anna smiled. "Lots of times."

"Me, too. It's the only secret I ever kept from you—how much I wanted that." Nessie lowered her head and moved to break their contact. "That's not true. I didn't tell you," she lifted her eyes to meet Anna's, "about imaginin' what it would be like if Rufus kissed me."

"Why not, Ness?"

"Remember when you told me about that one boy your Papa sent to courtin', and how he waited 'til your grandma left the room and then he kissed you?"

"I didn't like it, Ness, not at all. It was all slobbery, and he pushed so hard it felt like he split my lip against my tooth."

"I know, but I didn't like how it made me feel. I thought if I told you about Rufus, you'd feel that way, too."

Anna kept Nessie's eyes as she reached to cup the side of Nessie's face. She leaned forward and kissed her again.

This time when it took her breath, caught it and held it captive, it didn't surprise Nessie. She knew what kissing her would do, how the warmth of it would start there and then find its way to every part of her. Continuing, sparking, even after Anna lifted her lips.

"This is how I want to feel," Anna said softly, "only with you. Do you feel it, too?"

"Yes, I feel it, too," she replied. "It has to be a secret, though."

"It's all right, Ness. We won't tell anyone. It'll just be you and me, and the special way we feel."

20

The summer of denial morphed without much notice into the season of settling. It was an uneventful string of months, but for the horse backing the wagon over Nessie's papa's leg. He strapped boards on either side of his leg and hobbled on through the pain.

Responses to letters they'd written to families, provided by Miss Tilton and Mrs. Jenkins, started coming back and provided financial information and contacts to colleges in New York and Baltimore and Oberlin. Schools that admitted women, some that even admitted Negro women. But the more information they received, the more daunting the possibility seemed. The latest was a response from Johns Hopkins College. Anna opened the envelope with far less enthusiasm than she had the earlier ones.

"What does it say?" Nessie asked with a tone slightly more hopeful. "Is it the one in Baltimore?"

"Yes, Johns Hopkins." Anna sat quickly at the top of the back steps. Nessie sat close and peered at the open letter.

"That's a lot of money," Nessie said.

"Even more than Oberlin. But it's a good medical school, and Morgan College is right there for you." Anna stared at the letter. "We could both go to Oberlin, though."

"But you don't know if it has nursing classes."

"How are we going to get that much money, and enough to pay for a place to stay?"

"We'll write letters to people from the church in both cities. Miss Tilton said that some families have students live with them, and have 'em do chores to help pay for stayin' there."

"You find out where to send them, and we'll write letters, then,"

120

Anna replied. "First, though, I have to stash this letter with the rest." She rose and bound down the steps. "I'll tell Gram, but I can't take a chance on Emily finding it. She'd go right to Papa."

They tucked the letter safely in the box under the floorboards of their little house, counted the latest tally of money saved, and headed back to their homes early. They'd write their letters and compare them tomorrow.

The components were there for their plan to work, not as soon as they had hoped, but it did seem possible. The initial enthusiasm, though, had been severely tempered.

Anna struggled to hold on to the positives as she walked the path home. It was a thought-filled, move-by-rote amble until she was about fifty yards from the barn. She looked up to see the buggy parked at the top of the drive and Emily placing something on the back of it. By itself, nothing unusual. What caused Anna to stop where she was and watch was the way Emily turned her head from side to side as if making sure that no one was watching her.

Anna bent down among the tall grass. Who was using the buggy? Emily again? She'd already spent time with Papa yesterday. Emily had become quite strategic—if you actually go where you're supposed to be, when you're supposed to be there, then there is less scrutiny on other times, when at least some of them are spent behind the mercantile.

One more look all around and Emily left the back of the buggy and went into the house. Anna closed the distance to the barn quickly. Whatever Emily put in the back of the buggy was covered with a blanket, tucked tightly all around it. Anna glanced at the back door, saw no Emily, and decided to satisfy her curiosity.

She pulled the corner of the blanket free and looked under it. There wasn't much about Emily that surprised Anna, but finding her suitcase hidden under the blanket did. She lifted the end of it—heavy enough to be full—then tucked the blanket back in place and began an internal questioning that she hadn't prepared for.

Slowly Anna entered the house. Mrs. Jameson had left for the day. The dinner casserole was baking in the oven and fresh bread was cooling on the counter nearby. Gram would be rising from her nap shortly to finish by boiling the beans.

What did it mean exactly—the suitcase? Had Emily decided to stay at Papa's? A stay longer than one night if she needed a suitcase. Why hadn't there been discussion of it? Or maybe there had been. Anyway, Anna decided, treading lightly was probably best.

Anna started down the hall to her room when Emily emerged from the guest room. She seemed momentarily surprised, but recovered. "Just borrowing something of Momma's," she said, tucking whatever it was behind her skirt. "What are you doing home early? Have a fight with Nessie?"

Treading lightly. Always intended, always difficult. She stifled the desire to say the obvious. Had Emily ever known of a fight with Nessie? Of course not: she wasn't concerned with the obvious. She was doing what served her best—diverting.

Tread a little heavier. "Who's taking the buggy?"

"Why? Do you need it?"

"Maybe."

Emily had moved toward her room. "Today?" she asked without looking back.

"Gram's running out of white thread."

"Or, you're running out of white thread." She turned to face Anna and spat, "Those dolls. I should tell Papa how you're 'selling your wares'."

"I'm sure he knows."

"Not how many. Did you think I didn't know? And spending all your time with a Negro girl and making dolls for money instead of finding a husband. Do you think Papa hasn't noticed?"

"No doubt you made sure of that."

"Oh, not everything." She hadn't opened the door to her room, but stood as though waiting for Anna to leave before she did. "I haven't told him about you setting up house with Nessie. Something children do at play, but at your age? It's odd, Anna. Odd."

It wasn't a surprise, a little startling to hear it put into words, but no surprise that Emily would nose around. The only question had always been how long they could keep it from her. They had been mindful of not wearing an obvious path off the main one to the Jameson house, each time veering off at a different place. But somehow Emily found out, and now, Anna envisioned her sneaking into their little house, going through their books and papers. "It's really none of your business." Did she find the letters to the colleges, figure out their plan?

"Well, then, it's none of your business if I go into town today, is it?" She placed her hand on the knob, but didn't open it. Her tone lightened and she tilted her head. "I'll pick up your thread for you while I'm there."

Emily finally opened her door, slipped inside, and left Anna to decide whether to confront her about the suitcase or leave it be. She was clever, Anna had to admit. A confrontation had a clear consequence. One, she decided, not worth chancing.

By the time Grandma Addy rose from her nap to finish dinner preparation, Mr. Shakly had arrived to drive the buggy and had taken Emily to town.

"Anna, will you ask Emily to come down and—"

"She's not here, Gram. Mr. Shakly took her into town earlier."

Addy shook her head as she lit the flame under the pot of beans. "Where'd she say she was going?"

"She didn't say. Just that she would pick me up some more thread while she's there." One thing was clear now. Grandma Addy hadn't been privy to any discussion of Emily staying at Papa's.

Dinnertime, sitting across the large dining table from her grandmother, was fraught with indecision—tell her grandmother about the suitcase, or keep it to herself? Her secret was no longer her own. And her once-powerful ammunition against Emily could now only be used to block Emily's move—a stalemate.

Grandma Addy was unusually quiet. There was no summary of recent news articles, or asking about the most recent book Anna had read, commonplace dinner conversation. The quiet one at the dinner table was generally Emily—uninterested, bored, tolerating discussions only so long before rudeness offered her some sort of satisfaction. Strange how much she affected the conversation even when she was gone.

Anna cleared the plates to the kitchen and heard the buggy coming up the drive. She went to the door and watched as Mr. Shakly brought the empty buggy to the barn. There was no avoiding it now. Anna returned to the dining room to let her grandmother know.

"Anna, tell him that I need to talk with him."

Addy met him in the kitchen and settled as comfortably as she could on a stool. "Because I trust you intrinsically, John," she began, "I'm going to assume that you drove my granddaughter to town thinking that I had given permission, and that I knew where she was going."

"Yes, ma'am," he replied with an expression that verified both his assumption and his surprise at it being wrong. "I surely would have checked with you had I thought it out of the ordinary, Miss Adeline."

"Yes, yes, I know," she replied. "But now I need to know where she is."

"I took her straight away to Mr. Benson's just as she asked. She said that she had some things she needed to take to him."

"And you saw her safely in the door?"

"Oh, yes, ma'am, I sure did."

"When are you to pick her up?"

"She told me that Mr. Benson will see to her getting home. I'm sorry, Miss Adeline, if I—"

"No, John, don't worry yourself about it. It's her responsibility to discuss such things with me. I'm sure that Mr. Benson will take care of things from here."

John nodded and started for the door. "I'll be takin' care of the horse and buggy, and headin' home, then."

"Thank you, John."

Anna waited in the hallway until her grandmother said, "So, you heard. Come on in here."

She wrapped her arms around her grandmother's shoulders from behind, and kissed the side of her head. "You worry too much about us, Gram."

"No," she said, "never too much."

21

"The flowerbeds are beautiful, Anna," Addy said from the swing on the porch. "I don't remember them being so full and vibrant before you began tending them. They color the drab corners of even the plainest of days. Don't you think so?"

Anna straightened her back and dropped a handful of pulled weeds into the bushel basket next to her. "I do, Gram. They make you feel happy for just no reason at all." She dragged the basket by its handle around the corner and began working on the bed at the north end of the porch behind Addy's swing. "Momma would think they are beautiful, wouldn't she?"

"Yes, I think they would have brightened even her saddest days."

"Do you think she can see them, or somehow feels how much we want her to? Nessie thinks she can."

Addy stopped stitching and leaned back to let the swing move her in a gentle arc. "I dare say that your momma sees more now than she did when she was right here in the flesh."

"I wish there had been enough then to make her happy. I miss her."

"I do, too. Sometimes, though, something scary or sad looms up so large in front of you that you can't see around it to how bright and full of hope the day really is. If you step back away from it, you'll see how much smaller it gets, and you'll be able to see all the beauty getting bigger around it."

"What was it that Momma couldn't—"

"Adeline." It was a call this time, not a shout, as Thomas came through the house. "Adeline?"

"On the porch, Thomas," Addy called back. "Go on now, Anna. You've worked long enough on those weeds."

The message wasn't missed. Anna picked up the basket, moved around the side of the house, and stopped. She stepped between the plants and stood close to the building where she'd still be able to hear the conversation.

Thomas closed the screen door behind him, his demeanor calm and civil. He handed Addy a small, leather-covered journal, pulled a chair closer to the swing, and sat down. He leaned forward and asked, "What is this all about?"

Addy thumbed through the first few pages. "Mary's journal," she said. "Where—"

"It was on my desk in town. And this was with it."

The note he handed her was written in Emily's unmistakable cursive. Addy read it out loud. "I'll never allow anyone to do to me what you did to Momma."

"I loved Mary," he said.

"I know, Thomas. I know you did."

"It was her sickness talking there." He motioned with a weak turn of his hand. "Emily doesn't understand."

"No, she doesn't. You never took the time to talk with her about it. She needed you to tell her."

"The times when she would come in to town and spend time with me—I thought everything was all right."

"I've tried to tell you that she was using those times so that she could also claim that she was with you when she was actually spending time with the boy from the mercantile."

"Even after I forbid her? And I spoke with the boy's father. We have an understanding."

"Her mother's death affected her much differently than it did Anna. For a long while Anna blamed herself for doing things that made her mother sad or unhappy. But Emily searched for cause outside herself. She needed to know who was at fault, who to blame. It was easy for her to be angry with me for telling her what to do in place of her mother. And easy for her to accept Anna's self-abasement."

Addy stopped in a moment of realization. This was the first time Thomas had ever really listened to something she was saying. His brow was knotted tightly, his eyes searching hers. He was still, and present.

126

"But, it was more complicated with you, Thomas," Addy continued. "She not only needed you as a parent, she wanted *you*, and no one else, to validate her world. She wanted you to somehow make it whole again. The fact that no one could do that was beyond her then, but she needed to feel that you were trying."

Thomas rested on his forearms, and dropped his eyes from Addy's. He thought for a long, quiet moment. "When she read what Mary had written . . . I didn't realize." He straightened his posture and looked again at Addy. "Will you have her come down so that I can talk to her? I'll try to explain. I want her to know how much I loved her mother, and that I love her."

"She didn't let you talk with her about it?" Addy eased forward to get up from the swing, and took Thomas' hand to help her up. "I know how stubborn she can be."

"I haven't seen her, Adeline. I was gone until late last night. She must have used her key and left the journal while I was gone."

The timeline began clicking into place, and Addy's suspicions stood up hard against a moment of concern. "Mr. Shakly drove her to town early yesterday afternoon. She told him that you would see to her coming home."

"Why would she say that? She knew I wasn't going to be there."

"I think I know," Addy replied. "Anna?" she called as she neared the screen door.

"I'll get her," he said. "Sit back down."

At the sound of her name, Anna had scrambled to the back of the house and hurried in the back door, just as her father was coming in the front.

"Anna," he called. "Where are you?"

"I'm here, Papa. I'm coming."

"Come to the porch, please, your grandmother and I need to talk to you."

Anna stopped to catch her breath. The usual roil of stomach acids was absent. This time it wouldn't be her needing to defend herself or keep quiet when she wanted to shout back. Her grandmother was seated once again on the swing, her father beginning to pace, as she joined them on the porch.

Addy began. "Anna, Emily did not go to your father's yesterday, which leaves us with two possibilities. One, causing us a great deal of worry, is that something bad may have happened to her. The other, is that she may have lied because she wanted to be somewhere else. I'm hoping you might know something that will relieve our fears here."

"Well," Anna replied, grateful that it was her grandmother asking the questions, "I did notice that Emily had packed a suitcase to take with her. But," she added quickly, "I thought there may have been plans for her to stay at Papa's for a while."

"No." He said it in a tone that proved his sensitivity was slipping. "So, she lied."

"Wait, Thomas." A much more diplomatic tone from Addy. "Anna, is Emily still spending time with Wesley, the boy from the mercantile?"

Anna nodded. The thought was barely a conscious one, but if she didn't answer out loud, did it count? Retaliation from Emily was still possible, wasn't it? A frightening thought.

"Thomas," Addy said, rising again from the swing, "We need to make a trip to the mercantile."

It would be hours before they would be back from town, hours before she would know for sure what Emily had done. Something about the whole jumble of thoughts and questions, all of them swirling around what was happening and what it meant, made one singular need stronger than all the rest. More than needing the answers, and more than what those answers might mean, she needed to see Nessie.

Today was garden day. Anna weeding the flowerbeds and Nessie tending the vegetable garden. Since Anna's duties ended early, she knew she'd find Nessie still at work.

Anna stopped at the edge of the garden to watch, for just a moment, just because the sight made her heart jump so. So small was she, almost swallowed by the rows of plants, the garden an expansive space by comparison. Brown baggy pants, a good size too big, exaggerated the thin frame beneath. She was bent over at half her height, working,

128

always without question or complaint. Even at stand-up height, Nessie was small. While Anna had grown taller and filled her frame, Nessie had barely broken five feet, a deceptive size concealing a wiry strength.

But what Anna saw, standing there right then, was the answer to what had always made her wonder— the warmth and flesh and breath of it. Answered in that second when Nessie's lips touched her own. Confirmed each time now as their special time together, their special feelings for each other became more and more demanding.

Hurry, her heart whispered. "Ness," she called, and charged down the narrow path toward her. Nessie straightened, hands full of weeds, and flashed a smile, wide and anxious.

"I'll help," Anna offered. "How much more do you have to do?"

"No need," she replied. Nessie dropped the weeds in a basket, and jumped over rows to the edge of the garden. She quickly washed her hands in a bucket of water, dried them on the front of her pants, and started running.

A stride away from Anna, she said, "Race you," and turned up her speed.

Anna laughed and took the challenge, but she was no match. She was hampered by a skirt, and trying to catch a gazelle. Anna ran her fastest, even though it didn't matter who got there first. They were running to the same thing, couldn't wait for the same reason.

Anna burst through the door and into Nessie's arms. They laughed and hugged. "You're either getting faster," Anna said. "Or I'm getting pitifully slow."

"You're getting—"

Anna stopped her, covering Nessie's lips with her own. And then a series of kisses, easy and free. No questioning, no hesitation. Only what was special without the words. Only for each other. The way they knew it must be.

They tumbled to the cot, wrapped tightly in each other's arms. Their lips met with touches they knew, warm and soft, always needing more, and quickly deepened beyond. The feeling they had known, the one driving them to each other and daring the want for more, raced past its boundary.

Nessie slipped her leg into the loose fabric of Anna's skirt, pushed their hips together and clutched the heat between them. She stayed there, welcoming the heat, as the desire for more grew with each kiss.

Anna grasped the back of Nessie's head and pulled her into an open kiss—going where they hadn't been, deeper into the passion they didn't need to understand. They had no words for where they were going. None were needed.

Anna went there first, sliding her hand under Nessie's shirt, smoothing her palm over the bare skin. Exciting new sensations sparked under her touch. Anna's hand explored over the contours of Nessie's rib cage and the small mounds of her breasts. Nipples stiffened from the gentle fingers finding their shape.

Nessie wanted to give Anna all the same wonderful feelings, to bring her to the same beautiful place. She trailed tender kisses across Anna's cheek, and lifted her blouse from the waistband of her skirt. Her skin was flawlessly smooth, hot under Nessie's hand. Her breasts full and firm, and caressing them sent spikes of excitement through Nessie's body. She wanted to keep touching her, keep being touched. To keep the spikes shooting through to the center of her.

Anna's breathing quickened with her own, her hips moved against Nessie's. Nothing mattered except what they gave each other, what they shared that they had shared with no one else. Nessie's body glowed with a brilliance she'd never felt. When Anna found the center of the brilliance, the heat and the wetness, Nessie lost all thought. Her hands left Anna's breasts to circle her back, clinging to her as her body raced out of control. Anna's kisses seared across Nessie's face and neck, her fingers moved intently. Sounds escaped Nessie's throat at will, and she felt as though her body was about to explode. Should she stop it? Could she? Her hips pressed hard against the fingers, against Anna. She wanted to stay there in that glorious, beautiful place, where her world was centered and locked forever in a special bond with Anna. But in the next instant, all the wonderful sensations burst free. Nothing she had ever imagined compared to it. And it was hers now, hers and Anna's.

Anna trembled and squeezed her legs tightly around Nessie. "I felt it, too," she whispered. "It's beautiful."

Nessie caught her breath, and whispered back. "I never thought it would be like that—so strong and good."

"It's how we're supposed to love a man. I'm sure of that. But I never will, Ness. I never will."

"I only want to feel like this with you, too. This is all I want."

"Another secret," Anna added.

Nessie smiled against Anna's cheek. "I'm glad we're good at keepin' 'em."

"Do you think we will ever be free of them? Or will they always be just ours?"

"Just ours." Nessie nuzzled her face into the warm moist place just below Anna's ear. "How did you get done with your chores so fast today?"

"I only finished one flower bed," Anna replied, sitting up. She pulled Nessie with her to lean back against the wall. "She's done it," she said. "Emily packed a suitcase and left. We don't know where she is. Papa doesn't know where she is."

"She ran off," Nessie replied. "I'll bet you for sure, she ran off."

Anna nodded. "With that Wesley boy. Or maybe she's stayin' with his family because Papa didn't want her seein' him anymore."

"He wouldn't be stayin' with them if your Papa had that talk with his papa. They wouldn't want to make him more mad."

"This is going to sound terrible, but, I hope they don't find her. She'll tell Papa about our place, about us. She's been savin' it, just like I was savin' knowing about Wesley. Now, I've got nothing, and she's got nothing to lose . . . what would we do, Ness?"

The hope that she would find an answer in the deep brown eyes was fleeting. At best, they held resignation. There were no answers, only consequences—well known, born into, unavoidable consequences. What was left was hope, that almost desperate sense of maybe, and they both clung to it.

"I hope they don't find her," Nessie said.

Daniel Hayes' family had owned the mercantile for over thirty years. Stalwarts, rebuilding after the big fire, and one of the families so tightly bound to their business that they were rarely thought of separately. So the thought of Wesley Hayes dismissing his obligations and causing a family scandal was hard to imagine.

The discussion about to happen, the questions demanding answers, would be father to father, the accepted manner of dealing with such publicly sensitive matters. The real answers, though, the ones balancing between what ought to be and what is, would be Addy's to sort.

Daniel Hayes knew, the minute Thomas and Addy entered the store, that this would be a discussion for the back room. He greeted them without a smile, and avoided small talk.

"I talked with Wesley like I promised," he said, closing the storeroom door behind them. "I told him I expected him to do things proper, and go to you first, to make his case to you to court her proper. But she keeps comin' 'round here, and I don't know what more I can do."

"It's not with permission that she comes around," Thomas said. "That's why I'm here, to fetch her after she lied about where she was going. I'll be taking her home and we need to just keep this between us. No need for anyone else to know."

"She's not here, Thomas. It's been probably three days since I saw her."

"And Wesley? Where's Wesley?"

"He left after work yesterday to help a friend pick up a load of wood and unload it. I expected him back before now, but I haven't seen him yet. Must have taken longer than he thought."

Thomas set his jaw, narrowed his eyes, but Addy spoke first. "What friend, Daniel? I'd like to talk with Wesley, if you don't mind." Diplomacy first, her forte, not his. She needed to show Thomas that it would work. And it did.

A ride across town, and it didn't take long for their suspicions to be confirmed. It had taken Wesley only a couple of hours after work yesterday to help move a heavy load of wood. He just hadn't gone back home.

The quandary had begun. Who do you ask when you want no one to know of your suspicions? How do you quell your worries without sharpening a scandal?

"So, they're together," Thomas said, throwing his arms to his sides in frustration. "Aren't they?" He needed no answer, only to say it, solidify it, hang his anger on it. "Where are they, Addy?"

Needing to settle it in her own mind, Addy began to move the pieces of the puzzle. "Neither of them took a buggy," she said, "so they are either somewhere here in town, or they took the train."

"I want to hunt them down, Adeline. I want to bring her home and make this go away."

"You'll have to decide what's most important first. Start your hunt, and bring the conversation front and center, or let them be and let a quiet scandal die a natural death."

"I swear this family is steeped in scandal, born of it natural, I guess. Is this the price I pay for loving Mary?"

"I just see scandal as life not following the course others set for it. You could call it a number of things besides 'scandal', Thomas."

He turned to continue his pacing, starting back toward the front of the buggy. "Do you think they went North? If I knew, I could follow, and ask at each—"

"Have you thought that they might be happy together? Is there more that you would want for her?"

He stopped mid-pace, turned, and stared at Addy in the buggy. He said nothing until he had returned to the front and climbed into the driver's seat. "Is that what you want, Addy?"

In all the years she had known him, he had never asked. He had stated, demanded, but never asked. "And to know that she's safe," Addy replied. "Somehow. To know that she is happy and safe. I know of nothing more important."

22

The letter came two months later, Addy's wish fulfilled. It was stamped Greensburg, Indiana, and read in part, "We stopped in Dalton and had a young preacher there marry us. Wesley's going to be a preacher. A church family here is putting us up for now. I'll be a preacher's wife. We are very happy. Momma would be so pleased to know that I'll be accompanying the choir on the piano. Please tell Papa not to be mad anymore."

No mention of her sister's unorthodox behavior. No retaliation. No mention of Anna at all. The end of her grandmother's reading had sent a wave of relief over Anna. For two months she and Nessie had wondered, waited for what they assumed was inevitable. They had met each day in their house, loved each other cautiously at first, as if too much eagerness would prompt a letter faster. And then, as days became weeks, welcome white-hot blasts claimed every moment of need. They loved each other as if there would be no moment after, as though each time would be their last together.

And Thomas, after threading a needle's eye with his story of the couple traveling separately and being married by a friend in another city, could be pleased that he wasn't far from the truth. There could be satisfaction, too, in his daughter's role as a preacher's wife. She may not have married well monetarily, but she had married into social grace. Few would argue such a noble role. Yes, Thomas could lift a glass to the relief and enjoy a fine cigar in his daughter's honor. He had but one more marriage to worry about.

So he persistently sent the suitors, and they made their appearances in Grandma Addy's parlor. And just as persistently, Rufus Tinker used every excuse he could to make himself a Jameson household name.

Even with the reduced need for hands in the fields, the loss of the general workforce to the war and the exodus north left both farms with too few hands working too many hours. Rufus had become a welcome sight, taking up chores left undone. After the wagon accident, he had lent a hand to Nessie's papa to allow healing time. But months later, and despite every attempt to deny it, the leg wasn't healing. His lameness only increased, and his normal tasks became impossible. Now, barely able to walk, Calvin watched as Rufus pulled the last of the feedbags from the back of the wagon.

Calvin turned in the seat and rested his arm over the back as he spoke. "I'm sorry I can't pay you what your work is worth to me, Rufus."

"Don't worry none 'bout that," he replied, stacking the bag on top of the others. "This here's helpin' me, too."

"Your papa lookin' to get you into the Coca Cola plant with him?"

"Yes, sir. But if he does, I'll still be out here helpin' you out, too. I don't mind at all." Rufus also didn't mind catching a glimpse here or a word there of Nessie, or being invited for dinner where he could manage a fair amount of Nessie-watching.

And it wasn't that Calvin hadn't noticed. He was doing his own bit of watching—sizing up this young man, deciding his worthiness for his daughter. Some things seemed clear to the whole family: his heart was the biggest measure of him and there wasn't much in life that he couldn't find enjoyment in. Even Nessie had to admit that having him around wasn't a bad idea.

Of course, that meant a certain amount of avoidance was necessary. Nessie had to field sweet talk and marriage proposals that for Rufus were as routine as asking other folks how their day had been. And his hard-to-avoid interest posed yet another concern for Nessie: keeping her and Anna's little house a secret from him. They had only recently felt relief from Emily's threat and now they had to worry about Rufus.

Nessie made a point to know what chores Rufus was doing each day, and had gotten pretty good at estimating how long each took. Today, though, Nessie wasn't quick enough and avoidance wasn't possible. Ten minutes earlier, Rufus would have still been unloading feed in the barn and Nessie could have been out the door and safely out of sight. Instead, she was only a few steps outside the house when Rufus spotted her.

"There's my girl," he said.

She turned as he loped toward her, flashing a smile that captured and convinced with seemingly so little effort.

"How is it possible?" he said, circling around in front of her. "I swear, Nessie, you outshine the sun."

Nessie only smiled and shook her head.

"It just don't seem fair," he continued, "them flowers of your momma's, bright yellow as the sun, ain't got no chance at all a bein' as pretty as you."

"You're so full of mush, I bet you don't believe half of what you say."

"Swear it on a stack of Bibles this high." He raised his hand to the top of his reach. "I'd work here for your papa for no wage at all as long as I can see you every day."

"No need for that. Papa will pay you what he can. Much as he hates admittin' it, he probably will never be able to do the work he used to do."

"He got a lot a pride, your papa. He still talks like he won't need me once that leg heals up." Rufus stuffed his hands in the pockets of his old brown pants and offered a rare frown. "I sure won't never say it to him, but I don't see that leg's gonna heal. Like when a horse goes lame, it ain't never good for workin' after."

"That's right, Rufus Tinker, you keep them thoughts to yourself. He'll come to his own way of dealing with it. I just know that if it came to losin' this farm, he'd work it on one leg 'til he dropped. I know that for sure."

Rufus nodded, hands still deep in his pockets, his shoulders hunched up. "Don't you worry," he said, and eased into a quick, reassuring smile. "Ain't nobody gonna let it get to that. That's what's for sure."

"Now that I think you do believe," she said, stepping around him. "You'd better check see if Papa needs any more help today."

"Yeah, I got one more thing to do," he replied. "Where you off to, Nessie?"

"Got some things to do for Anna's grandma," she said, clearly on her way.

"Marry me tomorrow, then," he said in his *I'll let you decide how serious* tone, the one that always had Nessie shaking her head.

She shook her head, raised her hand, and called over her shoulder. "Gonna be pretty busy tomorrow."

"Hey, Ness." Anna closed the screen door behind her and joined Nessie on the back porch. "What's wrong? I was about to leave to meet you."

"We can't go, not right now." She took Anna's hand and pulled her down to sit on the top step with her. "Rufus was watchin', so I had to come up here instead."

"I was worried about Papa, and now you're worried about Rufus."

"'Was' worried? You said 'was'."

"Why can't we go away and just be together? It's been our dream all along, and Emily goes and makes it hers. It should be us, Nessie. Why isn't it us?"

"Where did they go?"

Saying it out loud only made Anna more irritated that Emily was the one up North. "She did what we should have."

"But we're not like Emily," Nessie said. "We couldn't leave and not worry about anyone else—just go and not tell our families. I didn't know that about us, though, until she left like that."

"Emily knew. It made it easier for her. She knew I would take care of Gram."

"What if we had left first?"

Anna shook her head. "She would have been so angry. I wouldn't have trusted that she'd care for Gram, or that she wouldn't retaliate. I think the only reason that she didn't say anything about us in her letter is that she got what she wanted."

"What do you think she knows?"

137

"I don't know," Anna said. "Enough."

"I don't wanna think about Rufus findin' out. He's there most every day now helpin' Papa . . . what would they do to us?"

"I don't want to think about that either."

23

The plan seemed a simple one—no meeting at the little house during daylight. Chores together during the day, visiting like friends do on the porch or back steps, wanting more and knowing better. Patience. They found patience to get them through each day, until they knew Rufus had left and they were safe to meet.

It was then, in the darkness of their own private space, that they ignored consequences, forgot about danger. Excuses now, and lying, had become routine in order to get out of their houses after dark. Each was always at the other's house, delivering this, working on that. As many nights a week as they dared. Each knowing what it meant to the other and how special their time was together.

"What if we could decide what our life would be like?" Nessie asked, nestling tighter against Anna in the darkness. "And our papas and people in the church would have no say, and no one would care if you are white and I am a Negro?"

"I wonder how women like Ida B. Wells and Anna Shaw live? Do people hate them, and try to control them?"

"But they're not like us," Nessie said softly. "No one's like us."

"No," Anna replied, and squeezed her arms tightly around Nessie. "No one."

Addy heard Thomas' heavy steps ascending the stairs, marching down the upstairs hallway, and back down again to appear in the parlor doorway. "Where is she, Adeline?"

In all the years, Adeline had never wanted free of this man more than she did right now. She had tolerated him, cared for her family in spite of him, and known all along that there was no other way. She had known since she was a young girl that her life would never be what society expected—not in her heart, not in her mind. But it hadn't taken her long to know that she had to find the line, the one that kept her on the right side of respectability. Finding it, though, had only started the bumping and nudging, the process of testing where the line could be moved without consequence. She sensed that tonight she was facing one more test of that line.

"She's taking something to the Jamesons."

"After dark? It couldn't have been done during the day?"

"I guess I don't understand the problem, Thomas."

"Exactly." He remained standing, an unspoken signal that Addy knew well. He was guarding the line, holding it steady. "There's a lot that you don't seem to understand, Adeline."

Addy placed her stitching on the table next to the rocker and leaned back. "What don't I understand?"

He pulled an envelope from his breast pocket and handed it to her. "This came today from Emily. I've tolerated your dealings with Negroes because I had no other choice. But you continue to stray from proper social behavior. Influencing other women to want to vote like a man and challenging society's rightful authority over Negroes only testifies to the need of a husband to guide you. You should have found another good man after the Captain's death. I couldn't change that. But Anna is my daughter, my responsibility."

His rant continued. Addy had heard most of it before. She ignored the condemnation, the implications, and read Emily's letter. What she read, narrow and bordering on vindictive, surprised her. Emily knew more than even Addy had suspected, and she had left Thomas with little room to doubt.

Addy took her first opportunity. "You must remember, Thomas, that Emily and Anna have never gotten along as sisters should. I don't know that you should take any of these accusations as anything more than Emily trying to push her way back into your favor. What better way to do that than to turn your disdain to Anna? The worse she makes Anna look, the better Emily looks."

"Are you denying that, after all our attempts to have Anna develop normal friendships with white girls, and all the perfectly acceptable suitors I've sent out here, she has dismissed everyone to spend her time with that Negro girl?"

"Dismissed? I wouldn't say—"

"Did you know about the old slave quarters?" His voice rose, touching the edge of his control. "About them spending their time together in there? My daughter, with everything she needs to attract a husband that will provide a home and children, holing up in slave quarters with a Negro girl. It's not right. It's not normal. And, I am going to put a stop to it."

Anna stood at the back door, hand frozen on the handle of the screen door. The sight of her father's buggy had surprised her, but it was the sound of his voice, the struggle for control, that stopped her. She strained to hear her grandmother's softer tone. To know if there was to be a taming of her father's ire. It was best, she was sure, to stay clear.

Addy rocked forward in the chair, and rose slowly. She stood as straight and tall as her joints would allow, and locked her eyes on Thomas's.

"You talk about tolerance," she began. "Well, I have a little experience with that myself. I've had to tolerate insolence and disrespect. Men and many women have dismissed my opinions and my decisions for the sole reason that I am a woman. My intelligence, my abilities, my resolve, all questioned and considered less than worthy because I am a woman. All things that you take for granted, that you accept as your birthright. You accept them without having to earn them. And yet, I am not afforded even the opportunity to earn those same rights."

"Are you through? Because none of that has anything to do with why I am here."

"Oh, it does," she replied, "but I doubt that you will ever be able to see it."

"I've allowed you to speak—"

"No. I spoke because I had something to say, not because I was allowed. I will speak as I wish in my home, and I will do what I can to make it so that some day other women will speak freely wherever they wish."

141

"You're a foolish old woman. And your foolishness is robbing my daughter of the life she is meant to live. You're leaving me no choice but to commit her to a hospital for help."

Addy knew that he had no idea what this foolish old woman could do, what she had done, once. And she wouldn't tell him, not yet, not unless there was no other option. Then, there would be no doubt in Addy's mind that she would stand her ground between him and Anna, shotgun in hand, and make sure that he never took her anywhere. First, though, she would exhaust her options.

"You know, Thomas, she hasn't been able to go to college like she wanted. Many women seem to find men more to their liking that way. Maybe if she had the chance to meet men on her own terms."

"I don't need to be having this conversation with you. I'm her father, and until she has a husband, what she does or does not do will be my decision."

Addy held her thought, muffled it safely before it took voice. She'd give him time. He needed time. Long enough to convince himself that it would indeed be his decision. How he got there didn't matter.

His stare was in Addy's direction, but he made no eye contact. A few seconds later, Thomas turned and moved decisively toward the doorway before stopping. He turned with a pointed finger and thrust it with emphasis. "One way or another, Adeline, I'm going to put her in a proper place—away from that girl and away from those damn Negroes."

Addy took a deep breath and released it slowly as she eased back into the rocker. No need for the shotgun tonight.

Anna waited, tucked out of sight around the back corner of the house, until her father left the house and his buggy was safely down the drive. What she had heard of the conversation was enough to know that it was about her, and that it was serious.

She entered the room quietly. Her grandmother was sitting in the rocker, her head tilted back, her eyes closed as if she were sleeping.

But as Anna approached, she saw a wet track of fresh tears along the softly wrinkled cheek.

"Gram," she said, and waited for the watery blue of her grand-mother's eyes. "Gram, are you all right?"

Addy wiped the wetness from her cheeks and sat upright. "I have to talk to you," she said. "And you must listen."

Anna sat at the end of the love seat closest to the rocker. "It's Papa, isn't it? I saw him leaving."

"There is nothing," Addy began, "within my power, that I wouldn't do to make sure that you are safe and happy. I want that more than anything. It is what I have hoped for, and prayed for, ever since you were born."

"I know, Gram. I've always known that. I can't imagine growing up without you."

"But there are things that I am not able to change," Addy continued, "no matter how much I want to. And, it's not going to be easy for you." The purity in Anna's eyes struck her, halted her thought for a moment, for a futile wish that she did not have to go on. That for the sake of what was good and right she would not have to taint that purity. But society would not allow it to remain, and neither could she. "I wish there was another way, Anna, but I don't know of one."

"What's happened, Gram?"

She is a young woman, Addy reminded herself—though older than Addy herself had been when Mary was born. Old enough to understand, strong enough to do what she must. "Your father was already unhappy with your lack of interest in suitors. But now Emily has written him about you and Nessie."

"It's not her business. What does she care? She has what she wants, why does she have to bother with me?"

"It's your father you need to be concerned with now. Anna, he was ready to send you to a mental hospital."

Anna's eyes widened. "I won't go. He can't make me go."

"He can. And I'm convinced that he would have. Just as Gladys Ashford's husband would have if she had not stopped coming to the meetings here."

"But why?"

"She was talking about things that he doesn't want her talking about. The meetings were filling her head with things that he thought women shouldn't be concerned with."

"She's supposed to think only what he wants her to? And if she doesn't, he can send her away? Why does he have that right, why can't she just refuse? It's not right."

"It isn't what is right, Anna, it's what is. Right or wrong only matters in the long suffering for change. In the meantime, we live within what is. It doesn't mean that we must accept it, or stop working for better. We should always work for better. But you must always understand the risks."

"So, if I refuse to live my life by his wishes—"

"By what is acceptable. We find the edge of acceptable. I planted the idea in his head to allow you to go to college. I told him that many women find men there more to their liking that way. We have to give him time to decide if he thinks people will see that as a more acceptable solution than the institution."

"And, if he does and I don't find a suitable man?"

"It gives you time, important time, to find another edge."

"What about Nessie?"

"She understands risks better than you do. You need to tell her."

"Would your papa ever come back here to see for himself?" Nessie asked.

They huddled together in their now compromised space, door barred and window curtain closed tightly. Anna's night had been filled with tears, her day fraught with bouts of anger and defiance. Her only relief came as she was finally able to see Nessie and spill the contents of last night's conversation.

"If he knew that I was defying him, yes."

Anna nestled her head in Nessie's lap, while Nessie stroked the silky hair pulled back over Anna's ear. "I heard about that mental hospital," Nessie said. "They shut you up in a room by yourself, and only your papa can say when you get out. People are left there for years. Sometimes they never get out."

"I'll never let him send me there . . . we should run, Ness," Anna said as she sat up. "Just up and leave like Emily did. We can. We'll take the money we have saved and take the train as far as we can."

"Church people put Emily up. Maybe we'll find someone, too. But what about your grandmother? Will your heart let you leave her alone?"

"If I go to school like she wants, I won't be here much anyway."

"You'd be able to come back home if she needed you. But if we go North . . . "

The worry would be heavy, useless, Anna knew that—sand in a grain bag, she'd carry it without purpose. "And what of us, Nessie? What will it do to our hearts if we can't be together?"

"The only thing that would hurt my heart more would be if being with you made your life worse than being without me. I would never hurt you like that."

"How could that be?" She took Nessie's face in her hands. "How could being without you ever be better than this?" Anna touched her lips to Nessie's, gentle touches, brushing over her lips and her cheek, warmly resting in the sensitive place below Nessie's ear.

"Never better," Nessie whispered, "only safer."

To own an idea that wasn't yours took time, long enough to put a convincing distance between its origin and your decision. And for Thomas, maybe longer than some. But he was a man with a dilemma and a chance to show that he could take control of a complicated and embarrassing situation and do what was right. A noble effort, to be sure.

There were plenty of men at the club ready with advice, some with personal experiences that gave Thomas serious thought. He had listened and weighed the possibilities, but it was George Wagner's success story that tipped the scale. He'd met his beautiful wife in college, where she'd learned to be one fine cook and manage a household that would make any man proud.

Two weeks later, he gave Addy his decision. Anna would have her chance to attend college, to make her life respectable. He would find a boarding house with rules that kept girls safe and respectable. And Anna would live by those rules.

24

Was it a reprieve, those days of indecision? Time still avoiding Rufus, still sneaking away to see each other, still waiting—for an answer to appear, neither of them voicing what they feared. It appeared to be. Yet, it floated precariously while the rest of the world swirled around it. A collision was inevitable.

Nessie tried her best to coax her grandfather into a few bites of nourishment. She sat at his bedside in the tiny room he had shared with her grandmother for as long as she could remember. He was so frail now, his health declining steadily over the past months. The once intense eyes now stared blankly, rarely registering with Nessie's.

"Just a bite, Grandpa," she said. But when the spoon touched his lips, he turned his head away. She placed the spoon back in the bowl, then smoothed her hand over his forehead and down his face, a bristle of gray stubble. "Okay," she said softly, "you rest. Maybe later you will feel up to eatin' somethin'."

She fought against the sadness and the tears, and started to leave the room. But the view from the doorway made her stop. Her parents still sat at the uncleared kitchen table. Her mother's arm was wrapped around her father's shoulders, her father's forehead rested heavily in his palms.

"How much?" Nessie heard her mother ask.

A muffled response from her father.

"It has to be a mistake," Willa replied. "We paid all that was owed."

Calvin lifted his head and this time Nessie heard his reply. "No," he said with a shake of his head, "it's no mistake. They can raise that tax whenever they want. They say we owe, we got to pay it."

"What are we going to do?"

"I talked with the bank about a loan, but they said we gotta figure a way to bring more money in."

"It's just the Negro farms, isn't it?"

Calvin pushed back his chair, and used the edge of the table to rise to his feet. "Don't matter if it is," he said, grabbing the cane from the back of the chair and limping from the room.

Nessie waited until he closed the bedroom door, then brought the uneaten bowl of food to the kitchen. "Grandpa wouldn't eat anything," she said, before looking at her mother. When there was no reply, Nessie turned to see her mother hurriedly trying to wipe the tears from her face.

"I know, Momma." Nessie knelt beside her mother and wrapped her arms around her. "I heard Papa say about the tax. Does Lewis know?"

"No. No one but you."

"They would take the farm, wouldn't they, if we can't pay it?"

Her mother's still teary eyes met Nessie's. "Don't say anything your grandpa can hear. He's gonna die thinkin' this land is his legacy to his children, and their children. We got to make sure of that."

No one needed to tell her that, just as no one needed to tell her what had to be done. She found Jackson and they took the wagon to Lewis's on the south end of the farm. Each of them on their own couldn't contribute much—Lewis with a family of his own now and Jackson already giving many free hours to the farm—but together maybe it would be enough.

So it was decided, without thought of consequence beyond a loss too great for the family, that Nessie's savings would go toward the tax. No one but Anna knew how much she had saved. No one but Nessie knew the true sacrifice. Emergency money she told them, put away for just this kind of situation. Such a smart girl, they said. The rest they would never know.

Anna was silent, sitting on the edge of their cot, staring ahead into the darkness. Nessie had tried to keep her voice steady, to deliver the worst possible news and not lose control. Tears streamed down her cheeks, but she told it all. Put to words the future they had both feared. Nessie swallowed hard, but it felt as though she was swallowing an egg whole.

Still, not a word from Anna. She stood and stepped to the window. The moon was bright, illuminating the white cotton curtain and outlining Anna in silhouette. Her silence didn't matter. Nessie knew Anna better than anyone—her fears, her hopes, her obstinacy. She had reasoned with her heart, dreamed without compromise, believed the impossible. Until now.

Anna's words were barely audible. "You've given away our future." That was all. Nothing more before she left, closing the door behind her and leaving Nessie to cry alone.

The pain was worse than any other in Nessie's life. Face down on the cot, she buried her sobs in the old pillow. It was the hardest thing she would ever have to do, she was sure of it. But how would she bear it?

What have I done? Made the decision without her. Hurt her. Turned away my sweet Anna. "Oh, Anna, I'm sorry. I'm so sorry." *Would it matter if I told her? If I ran to the house, refused to leave until I saw her, and told her how sorry I am, how I don't know what else to do? Would she believe me? What would it matter? She was right, I threw it all away.*

PART III

1918

25

Dearest Anna,

Your letters warm my heart. I am so proud of how well you are doing in your studies. You will make such a fine nurse.

I have heard nothing from your father of late, but I suppose that is to be expected. He has no cause to come out here now, as long as you and Emily are not here. Choose carefully what you tell him of your activities, and be mindful of being seen in the right places with the right people. It is for your welfare that I say this. Leda mentioned that you have attended suffrage meetings. As strongly as you know I believe in the vote, I must ask you not to attend. I will continue to speak out and support the movement because I bear the lesser risk.

You have never asked, and I have hesitated until now, but I feel obligated to tell you. Nessie married Rufus Tinker. Mrs. Jameson said that they just went to town one afternoon and had the Justice marry them. Nessie wanted no fuss, or for her family to spend any money. I offered to give a reception party for them, but Nessie refused. She still comes here to check on my well-being. I suspect, though, that she comes as much to check on you. Each day she asks if there is a new letter. She likes to have me read them to her. I suggested that she write you, but she said that she is sure that you would not want that. Anna, I wish that you would write to Nessie. You need to talk to each other. There is so much that you do not understand.

Although I love your letters, I truly miss seeing your sweet face. Being able to see you will make me very happy, and young Shakly has offered to drive me to church on Sunday.

So, until then I will send my love.

Grandma Addy

Rarely had there been anything her grandmother asked of her that Anna refused to do. Little things, growing up, inconsequential requests that had gotten ignored or forgotten, but nothing that she sensed was important, even if she didn't understand it at the time. Her grandmother's wisdom was something she never questioned.

This time, though, her grandmother didn't know what she was asking. This was a hurt that even thinking about made it painfully fresh again. The love she felt could not be explained. No one would understand it or accept it. It had been their secret, and now it belonged only to Anna.

Today, Leda insisted on meeting her at the hospital, a safe encounter delivering quilts that would go unnoticed by Anna's father. They settled in a small empty waiting room, where Leda wasted no time on general chatter.

She smiled a quick greeting, and began. "Your situation is nothing to take lightly, Anna. I know how you want to be a part of making this change happen. It's important. It will determine our future. But you must think of yourself right now."

"It's all I can do to stay quiet when I'm dismissed. Every day I am expected to accept, without question, someone else's idea of what my life should be like. But at the meetings, I am surrounded by women who feel like I do. They want what I want. There is nowhere else where I feel that support."

Leda nodded, with a look of knowing that offered needed reassurance to Anna. "It will come, Anna, just be patient. We are so close now. We've gained in numbers, and men like my husband are speaking publically in our favor. Leonard Grossman has formed the Men's League for Women's Suffrage. But the closer we get to the vote, the harder people who oppose it will fight. They fear losing control, and that kind of fear is dangerous."

"And if we don't get the vote, will I have to always be fearful to speak out? If I choose not to marry, will my life be governed by my father?"

"We will get there. I am more convinced now than I have ever been. Right now, though, you should be more concerned about being committed and losing all control of your life. Your grandmother and I don't want to tell you what to do, but please let those of us who can risk it, fight the visible battle. My husband won't commit me. He'll bail me out every time they throw me in jail. There is little that I am afraid of. Let us do it."

"What can I do?"

"Write," Leda replied. "Pen your support under another name. Send letters to all the newspapers, not just the local ones. And send them to mayors and councilmen and congressmen. Send them to the President. You never know whose heart your words might touch."

Yes, she decided on her walk back to the boarding house, she would write. That she could do—pour out all of the things she wished she could say out loud, about the injustice, and all of the contributions that women could make if only they were allowed. All those things she would say to her father if she could. And, more than that, she would fill every moment left empty by Nessie. She would study, volunteer at the hospital, and she would write.

She began putting the words together in her head as she walked, rearranging them, tempering them, leaving out those tinged with anger or frustration. Her pace quickened, up the walk to the steps, through the door; she wanted to get her thought on paper right away.

The parlor, though, was a buzz with familiar chatter and giggles. Helen, another border, and her cousin Celeste, spotted her and made avoidance impossible.

"Anna," Helen called. "Oh, I am so glad you got back before we left. You must come with us."

Anna stopped in the doorway. "No, I really can't. Not tonight. I have a lot of reading to do."

Helen offered a smile that Anna had begun to loathe. It meant that "no" was not an answer and that whatever it was that they were planning would include Anna regardless. Before Anna could say another word, the books were taken from her arms, and Celeste had hooked her arm through Anna's.

"If we don't drag you out of here from time to time," Celeste said, "I swear you will become a stuffy old maid."

"All that studying," Helen added with a giggle, "you must be planning on marrying a professor."

They had ushered her out the door before she could ask, "Where are we going?"

"The new theater," Helen said.

"The Rialto," Celeste added, jumping on top of Helen's words almost as they were spoken.

Helen: "Mary Pickford."

Celeste: "Oh, don't you love her?"

There was really no need for Anna to respond. The cousins chattered on, finishing each other's sentences and giggling about leading men and rumors of who Mary Pickford was in love with. Chatter that became a backdrop for Anna to insert her Oh, yeses and reallys every so often.

"Our treat tonight," Helen said as they approached the theater entrance.

It was grand, with its colorful new sign and pretty lights. One of so many new buildings revitalizing downtown Atlanta after the horrible fire the year before. People still talked about how it had started in the hospital warehouse where the mattresses were stored, and the other fires that broke out in other parts of the city. Hospital staff still talked about the buildings collapsing, and working the first aid stations.

Anna tried to hand Celeste the ten cents for her ticket, but it was refused. "No," Celeste said, hooking her arm with Anna's again. "It's our idea to force an afternoon of entertainment on you. Come on."

They turned their tickets in to the young man in the vest and pillbox hat in the lobby, and were directed to the theater door. A young Negro man, sweeping near the door, straightened and moved clear of their path.

"Little John," Anna said quickly. The sight of his face and a much-

156

needed sense of familiarity let his name slip into the open without thought. She saw her mistake immediately in his eyes.

He offered no expression in return. His eyes shifted to the cousins and back to Anna. "Ma'am," was all he said.

She couldn't take it back. And it made her angry that the thought she needed to had even entered her mind. She hated this, hated that it was expected of her to ignore someone she had known all her life, to treat him as something less than he was.

"What are you doing?" Helen asked. She grabbed Anna's arm and pulled her toward the door.

Anna offered one last look that she hoped Little John would understand, a quick nod, and turned away.

Little John lowered his eyes, offered another, "Ma'am," and turned away. With a few long strides, he disappeared around a corner.

"Well," Helen said as she grabbed Anna's arm again, "you are just lucky we're here. Talking to a Negro like that. There's no telling what he would have done if we weren't here. What made you do such a thing?"

"He used to work for my family," Anna lied. She looked directly at Helen and couldn't stop from adding. "He has always been respectful and loyal."

"You are quite naïve." Celeste sounded less like herself, and more like what Anna imagined her mother must sound like. "You can never trust a Negro, Anna, especially a Negro man."

She had let them chatter on over the months that she had known them. She'd tolerated their mindless following of opinions she disagreed with and let their offensive attitudes go unchallenged. It seemed fruitless, a waste of effort to argue the points with two women so set in the attitudes of society.

But this time it was so much harder to hold her tongue. This time they were taking away her familiar, making it something that it wasn't, making it personal. Anna struggled but remained silent, offering the cousins only a steely stare.

"Well, I'll not let you ruin the afternoon," Helen replied. "Come on, Celeste."

They moved on, found their seats, and left Anna to follow.

This, she acknowledged reluctantly, was where she was supposed to be. The right people, the right place.

The purging began the moment Anna closed the door to her room behind her. Tucked away in the small room, she sat at the writing desk next to the bed, and let the words cleanse away the sense of powerlessness that had dominated the afternoon. It wouldn't matter how many letters, or how long it would take her to write them, sleep wouldn't be possible anyway.

The list of names and addresses that Leda had given her grew weekly. Each night she continued to make her way down the list, and when they'd all received a letter from Claire Walker, she would start again at the top. She was a persistent woman, that Claire Walker.

Anna smiled as she signed her fourth letter, folded it, and sealed it in the envelope. Before she could begin the next, though, there was a knock on her door.

Mrs. Powell smiled only when it was expected, a period at the end of a sentence. And her unbending house rules made living here her father's perfect choice. "I won't keep you long, Anna," she began, "it's nearly bedtime. But I must talk with you about what happened this afternoon."

"This afternoon?" Nothing registered as a rule break or anything warranting a personal chat with Mrs. Powell.

"Yes, Helen came to me, quite concerned, and I must say she certainly has the right to be." She hesitated for a moment, but didn't seem to need a response. "Anna, you must learn to recognize a dangerous situation and react to it appropriately. If a Negro man approaches, or attempts to speak to you, you should move immediately to the safety of other whites, a man, preferably. He can assure that the Negro is dealt with."

"Oh, at the theater. I'm sorry," Anna said. "He was someone who used to work for my family."

"Here in the city, Anna, you are not dealing with field hands and servants who know their place. Familiarity can not be tolerated."

Though her words had progressed from warning to judgment, her tone never changed. "And you must never put your friends in danger again." Still that same educational tone. Mrs. Powell's social classroom.

"Yes, ma'am." A softly said reply, the only reasonable reply. Anything else would be reported to Papa.

Mrs. Powell smiled. The end of the sentence. "Good night, then."

"Yes, good night, Mrs. Powell."

The chastisement—Mrs Powell's, anyone's—wasn't necessary. It took only a few thoughtful moments, sitting quietly alone, to understand that what had happened this afternoon was about far more than the cousins.

It was so much more than that, reaching beyond it to what she had been unwilling to accept—that she would not be free to live by her own values. She had never wanted to accept it, never wanted Nessie to accept it, but today made it clear that there was no denying it. *Nessie was right, it's just how it is.*

26

The right people in the right places for too many months had proven two things to Anna. She needed the camaraderie and support of women who wanted the freedoms she wanted, and—no matter how much she had hoped differently—it had only emphasized her longing for Nessie and what could never be.

She lost track of how many letters she had written. It was a worthy mission, but not one capable of replacing the faces and voices of the women at the meetings. Nothing could replace the sound of the words, the way they took over the room, filled it, governed it. They painted a world she wanted to live in. The strength of them bolstered her hope, and carried it until she heard them again. As much as she said them in her mind, over and over, and wrote them with all the strength her words could convey, it wasn't enough.

Anna dropped today's batch of letters at the post on her way to the hospital and she counted on the children to lift her spirits. This week, the task would fall to the Negro children. As soon as she entered the ward, she felt it. Little gasps and squeals of anticipation lightened her heart and brought a smile that mirrored itself on all their faces. They knew what was in her book bag even before the nurses wheeled in the puppet theater. For this little while, Anna knew, happy children would be the best medicine for everyone.

The children settled at the foot of their beds on both sides of the center aisle so that they could see. Some hugged pillows and peered between the rungs; some rested their arms on the foot rails, and all focused intently on the antics of their favorite puppets. Today, puppets Mavis and Junie were sure that the pranks being pulled on them were at the hands of the clown, whose special hiding place was somewhere in the hospital.

Anna had them waiting for the next trick, laughing at the elusive clown. And they had her, working two hand puppets at once, ducking one down for the appearance of the clown. Filled with the joy of their laughter, her earlier reservations gone, she knew Nessie would have loved the new twist to their story.

She had been sure that she'd never be able to do the little theater again, that it would be too much of a reminder of what she had lost. And it had taken almost a year before she tried it, a special treat for a child who was going home against all the medical odds. And what she had learned was not at all what she had expected.

Here behind the theater, working the puppets, she felt so close to Nessie. She heard Nessie's inflections of the puppets' words in her own voice, felt the presence of her shoulder nudging up beside her. And every once in a while, she was sure she could smell the scent of her.

Putting on the puppet shows became her connection to Nessie. That's where she felt her, entertaining the children together once again. The stories were as familiar as the day they made them up, so much of Nessie in them—happy, hopeful. Her Nessie for as long as the story lasted.

But they were always over too soon. Her puppets, Mavis and Junie, took their bows and Anna emerged from behind the theater to take her own. The lift, Anna hoped, aided by the children's applause, would carry her into the evening and into a good night's sleep.

One of the nurses was making good on her promise for another special treat, and rolled in a cart filled with bowls of ice cream.

"You bring such blessings to the children, Anna," Dr. John Morgan spoke from behind her. "I can't tell you how much this is appreciated."

Anna smiled and tucked the puppets back into her book bag. He hadn't missed a day of the Little Theater performances, in either the Negro or white wards, and never failed to thank her. "My best friend and I started entertaining the younger ones when we were ten. I guess I can't think of a better way to bring that kind of joy." She turned back to the rows of children. "I love the look on their faces."

Dr. Morgan looked with her. "All of them are experiencing some sort of discomfort or pain, but I'll bet not one of them have felt a bit of it for the past hour."

"I wish I could do more," she replied. "I will do more."

He stepped up beside her. "What do you see when you look at those faces, Anna?"

The space between her brows pressed into a crease. The children were savoring their cold treats. "Strength," she said, "that doesn't seem like it should be there. And, something else," she turned to look at the doctor. "Is it trust? What is it that allows them to breathe in the probability of tomorrow without question?"

He looked at her, hazel-brown eyes focused intently. "You make me wonder as well," he said. He broke his focus with a smile. "I normally have an early dinner just down the street at Graham's. Would you join me today? I would really like to talk with you more."

There was no reason to refuse. Missing mealtime at Mrs. Powell's meant missing out on promised boredom at best. The doctor was young and courteous and smart, and just to make it that more difficult to say no, he was interested in what she had to say.

"Yes," she replied, "I'd like that."

Nothing fancy, he told her, but a restaurant that felt more like home to him. Simple wooden tables, quiet conversation, and the smells from an open kitchen welcomed them. A waitress he knew by name brought handwritten menus to the table.

"I love the chicken-fried steak casserole," he said. "It's as close to my grandmother's as I've ever tasted."

Anna looked over the other choices: potato bake, chicken cobbler, sweet potato casserole. "I think I'll try your recommendation," she decided. If it were anything like Mrs. Jameson's, it would be a good choice.

With the waitress gone, John folded his forearms and leaned forward on the table. "So, tell me," he began, "why do you want to be a nurse?"

No one had ever asked. Nessie knew. Grandma Addy knew. But no one else had cared enough to ask. "It's what I can do to make a difference. Isn't that why you became a doctor?"

"I've never been able to explain it that succinctly, but yes, that's exactly why." He leaned back in his chair and said, "Once I realized that the cinema already had a Douglas Fairbanks, Jr., and baseball had a Ty Cobb, it narrowed the choice considerably for me."

His expression had been deadpan serious, and it took Anna a moment to recognize his humor. He was nice enough looking, although probably not leading man material, and everyone seemed aware of the special shoe he wore to make his limp less noticeable. Both were easily overcome by his compassion and the respect that he paid those he worked with, both white and Negro. And, Anna could now add, his humor.

She ended a genuine smile with, "I'm meeting a lot of people who think you made the right choice."

He nodded and replied, "I love working at Grady. And as soon as you graduate and there is an opening, I know that you will, too."

"What makes you so sure?"

"What you didn't see when I asked you to tell me what you saw in the children's faces. You would have said the same thing had I asked that question in the white children's ward, wouldn't you?"

"Of course: they're all children."

"Exactly. And an injury is an injury, an illness is an illness. That's what I see."

"I wish there were more people who feel like you do."

"A lot of people working at Grady do. But I think there is a lot to be said for how you are raised," he said. "When you are allowed to get to know someone who you think is different than you, you soon find out there are far more ways that you are alike. You see their abilities and their talents, and they see yours. You realize that the same things make you happy or sad. Respect comes easy then." He stopped as the waitress brought their dinners. "I'm sorry. I didn't mean to monopolize the conversation."

"No. I'd like to hear more. I was raised in a complicated family. There were conflicts, there still are, about what is acceptable and what is not. I can only claim choosing what felt right to me. I'm curious to know how others have come to think the same way."

"It was easy for me," he began. "I don't ever remember making a choice. I lost my father when I was four. My only memory is of a tall man lifting me to his shoulder and carrying me about the yard. My mother never married after his death. She hired a Negro man, Frank, to keep up the house and yard. I grew up with his boys, and he was as much a father to me as anyone could have been." He slid his foot out from beneath the table and motioned to it. "Frank figured out how to build up a shoe for me. He saw me running along a board that was lying on the ground with my short leg on the board. I was running back and forth as fast as I could. It was the first time that he had ever seen me run. He said it just made sense to make my shoe as high as the board and then I could run anywhere I wanted. He never had any formal education, but that man could solve any problem you handed him. He changed my life in so many ways."

"He has a lot to be proud of." Anna watched him smile, one she imagined was meant for Frank.

"I hope so," he said, then held up his hand. With a quick shake of his head, he added, "Now I am going to stop. I've talked enough about myself. I want to know more about the new nurse Grady is going to have."

The sense of apprehension wasn't expected. His initial interest, those first questions had been welcome. An opportunity to be heard, to talk on a personal level with someone of the doctor's stature. A compliment that said that what she thought had merit. Then something changed—an expression, an inflection in his voice, she couldn't pinpoint it. But whatever it was made her hesitate.

"She's hungry," Anna said and grinned. "We'd better eat while our dinner is still warm."

27

With the exception of Anna's absence, nothing about the little house had changed. Nessie kept it swept and dusted, and fluffed the old feather pillow each time she left.

It was still her private place. She read there, the newspapers and books that she got from Grandma Addy, and she wrote letters that she would never send to Anna.

Early in the afternoons on the days that her momma delivered laundry and Rufus worked his shift at the Coca Cola Company, Nessie slipped away to her private place. Once a place filled with hopes and plans and dreams of the future, it now safely held her memories and her secrets. Maybe her little one, she thought, caressing her firm protruding belly, will play here someday. Maybe new dreams will find life here, voiced with excitement, bouncing with hope. And maybe, those dreams would someday be real.

Nessie turned the chair sideways to the table and placed her paper on the scrap end of wood that had become her writing board.

> Dear Anna,
> I don't know why this day has been worse than others. Every day I am without you is sad in so many ways. But I will never tell you of it. My sadness is a selfish thing beside the hurt I have caused you. Today, though, I have to write down my sadness. I need to take it from my thoughts and put it on paper so that I can look at it. Thinking about it isn't the same as looking at it.
> It makes me sad to know that I can't see your smile, or hear your voice. When I am alone in our place and I

close my eyes, sometimes I can hear your laughter. And when I press my face into the pillow I am sure I can smell you here. I know I will never hear you whisper to me in the dark again, or feel you so close to me that I can't tell where I stop and you begin.

I gave all of this away, just as you said. And when I write it down, it looks so small next to the look I saw in your eyes that day. I knew the second I saw it I would never be able to take it back or erase the hurt I caused you. That is my biggest sadness.

I know two things as sure as I know the sun will rise and set. Waiting for me would have cost you everything, and I will never feel for anyone what I feel for you.

Nessie folded the paper and tucked it into the wooden box with the others. She pushed the box as far back into the hole as she could, and replaced the floorboards.

It helped, she was sure it did, writing it down, making something more of her thoughts. One day maybe she would be able to take them from her secret place and destroy them. For now, though, she needed them right where they were, added to the others with the memories she never wanted to lose. Right there where she could add the whys on top of the hurt and the sadness—explain the reasons to Anna, to herself. Write them down like she had the rest, because someday they might finally be enough.

Until then, she would write what she couldn't say to anyone. She'd write it for as long as it took, while she lived the life she must.

Evening hours sitting in the parlor with Grandma Addy had quickly become Nessie's favorite time of the day. She nibbled a warm piece of cornbread, happy that Grandma Addy loved her momma's recipe as much as Anna did. She loved sharing the time here, reading and talking about things that were not discussed at home. Here, she found, challenging the status quo was not only acceptable, it was encouraged. Challenges, though, as Nessie knew well, had their limits.

"I have more articles for you, Nessie. More recent ones from Chicago." Addy gathered two papers from the table next to her rocker and handed them to Nessie.

"Do you think they would have lynched her," Nessie asked, "if Miss Wells had stayed in Tennessee?"

"Good chance," Addy said. "It was too much of a risk, to be sure, for her to stay South. But she has a voice that can ring out from wherever she is. She knows that."

"I wish I could be more like her. I read about brave women speaking out and trying to make changes, and I wish I could, too."

"You know Miss Tilton's group of women has grown and become a strong voice against lynching. *And* to get the women's vote. Have you talked with her lately?"

"Not for a long time, since Momma found out she was givin' me Miss Wells' writings. You know how my family feels."

Addy nodded. "And I would never judge what is best for them, or for you. I question whether I can even judge what is best for my own girls. Each of us has to figure out what will make us happy."

"What if what makes you happy just can't be?"

"Oh, dear Nessie." Addy leaned her head against the back of the chair and released a long sigh.

Addy's struggle was apparent. Rarely without thoughtful comment, she was thinking and hesitant, and Nessie sensed it. It was Billy she was thinking of, surely it was. *How do I tell her that I know, that I understand, that you need her.*

"If it can't be," Nessie said, "does it mean it was wrong to want it?"

Addy looked into Nessie's waiting eyes. "I don't know if this old woman can answer that. I searched for a long time, but I can't claim to have found an answer."

"Will you tell me what you thought about? I need to know."

"Of course you do." Addy reached out her hand and Nessie slid closer to the end of the love seat to take it. "It was many years ago, but I still remember how much I wanted someone who I could talk to, even if there were no answers. I needed to be able to tell someone how I felt, how conflicted I was. But there was no one." She squeezed Nessie's hand. "So, I know."

She wished Grandma Addy did know, about her and Anna, and how right it felt to love her. That's when she would understand what couldn't be, and why there would never be anyone for her to talk to either. Not about that.

"There was something I wanted," Addy began, "more than eating or sleeping. It was a love, Nessie, that filled me with such happiness that I was sure that I could endure anything for it. But I didn't know what that would mean. I suppose there was no way to know the consequences at the time. But they were devastating." The pale blue eyes glistened with a watery film, but there were no tears. "Was it wrong to want what once had brought such happiness?"

"But you didn't know," Nessie replied. "How could it be wrong if you didn't know that something horrible would happen?"

"That's the answer I've always tried to believe. I needed to, because to question it or to think differently was too painful."

Nessie's focus fell to their hands, still clasped and resting on the arm of the rocker. Her vision, though, was of a young soldier dying at Addy's feet. The sadness. The consequence. The one she couldn't have known.

"I don't know if I've been able to help with what is worrying you, Nessie. It seems to me that deciding what is right has to come from your heart, just as it came from mine."

And knowing what can't be, Nessie decided, tells your heart what must be. She nodded as Addy squeezed her hand once more before releasing it.

"I have a letter from Anna," Addy said with a lift to her voice. She retrieved the envelope from the table and unfolded the letter. "I haven't read it yet. I waited to share it with you."

The mention of Anna's name flickered and sparked in Nessie's chest. She took a deep breath as Addy donned her glasses and lifted the letter from her lap.

My dear Gram,
I hope this letter finds you well. There is so much illness

here in the city, and all across the state. The influenza out-break is being called an epidemic in the northeastern states, and the quarantine of Camp Gordon has helped to slow the infestation of the city. But there are more and more cases showing up now, over a hundred a day reported. With so many trained nurses needed at Camp Gordon, student nurses like me have been called to fill the need in the hospitals.

Do not dismiss early symptoms like a sore throat or a fever for a cold. It turns horrendous fast, with skin becoming a gray-blue color, nosebleeds, and difficulty breathing due to blood-tinged fluid filling the lungs. They don't know what causes it. It has hit so hard and moved so fast that there has been no time for developing a vaccine. All we can do is treat the symptoms, bring the fever down, and make our patients take nourish-ment. If anyone shows even the slightest of symptoms, keep them away from others and bring them here.

This is a serious situation, Gram, and it is very important to avoid coming to town until the disease is contained. The Board of Health has taken preventative action by closing all schools, churches, and places of public entertainment. Please tell Mr. Shakly to keep his workers from coming to town, and make sure that the Jamesons do the same. Nessie must be especially careful. If anyone in her family gets sick, tell her she must stay in my room. I was going to be there to help with the delivery, but I dare not now. Do watch over her for me. I worry so.

I have done as you asked, and what I must, associating with people who would give Papa no cause. But it has been tiresome. There are few I would spend time with if I were given the choice. I must say I welcome the many hours required of me at the hospital. I have no time or energy now for social silliness. Even Papa must realize my contribution.

Leda Jenkins's group of women will be joining another march for the vote. I should be with them. But I will write more letters tonight to ease my mind before I retire.

I send my deepest love and my hopes for your continued health.

Anna

Addy folded the letter and removed her glasses.

"She was going to come home to help me?" Nessie asked.

"Does that surprise you, Nessie?"

It shouldn't, Nessie thought. Anna had been her best friend all her life. What else would her grandmother think? It would be the most natural thing in the world for a best friend, a nurse, to do. Whatever Grandma Addy sensed, whatever disagreement or hurt she thought had happened between best friends, wouldn't be enough to keep Anna from being there at such a special time. And maybe she was right.

"She said that she's worrying about me."

"Of course she is. You don't stop worrying about someone you care about just because you're apart."

The thought made Nessie smile. Even if only for tonight, she would let Grandma Addy's words fill her heart.

"And she's right to worry about your family, too. You will emphasize the dangers to them, won't you?"

Nessie nodded. "Papa already has Rufus delivering the laundry for me and Momma. The Coca Cola Company cut Rufus' shift. They cut back hours because of the war restrictions on power. So we got to do all the laundry we can now."

"I worry that you may be doing sick people's laundry, though, Nessie."

"Momma don't think there's much danger doin' it outside in the fresh air. When you write to Anna, will you tell her not to worry?"

"I think it's time for you to tell her," Addy replied, "don't you? Write her, Nessie. Tell her how you feel."

The room didn't feel like hers, it probably never would. Nessie pulled back the covers on her grandparents' bed, removed her robe, and draped it over the chair. It made perfect sense for her and Rufus to move from her tiny room after her grandfather passed, but it didn't feel right.

The urge to start a letter to Anna, one that she might actually send, had bothered her since returning from Grandma Addy's. But, she couldn't write it here. It would have to wait until tomorrow and her next chance for privacy.

Nessie eased onto the bed, pushed an extra pillow between her knees, and tried to get comfortable. Tonight she would let the thoughts arrange themselves, and sort through them until she made sense of them, or she fell asleep trying. What should she say, how should she say it? She would decide tomorrow if there would be a letter or not.

The smell woke her before she felt Rufus crawling into bed behind her. His clumsy attempt to not wake her was made worse by the amount of alcohol he'd consumed. Every night now, she could count on him losing his balance, bumping into the bed, and then shushing himself as if it made his coming home so late less noticeable.

It hadn't bothered her at first, his stopping after work and drinking a few before coming home. But when his shift was cut, he began stopping at his cousin's after delivering the laundry, and staying past dinner. And then, this week he hadn't made it home until after she was in bed and asleep.

Her mother's explanation was, "some men gotta do that when their woman's with child." There didn't seem reason to question it, he wasn't shorting Papa on work, or doing anything worse than waking her. He was still sweet, maybe even sweeter, cuddling against her, nuzzling her neck, and smiling as he fell asleep. What had been unexpected, though, was the change to their intimacy. Nothing more than nuzzling and a gentle kiss was a change Nessie welcomed.

He had always been gentle, right from the first time. There had never been a doubt that he loved her, that he would do anything to make her happy. And in some ways he did make her happy. The way he looked at her, the sappy things he said, made her feel attractive and appreciated. She liked his fun-loving nature, and his respect for her parents. She loved the goodness of him. But, she did not love him like she loved Anna. And that he would never know.

28

The letter, the one that had started falling into place in Nessie's mind, had to wait. Birthing, without regard for daily routines or intended plans, had its own schedule. Contractions had begun before Nessie could put pen to paper, and priorities then set themselves.

Grandma Addy sent the news to Anna—a tiny, perfect baby girl after six hours of labor. Nessie's momma and sister-in-law took good care, and Nessie was fine and resting.

It took the better part of four months, now near the end of January, before a letter arrived at Anna's boarding house. The number of influenza cases had declined temporarily, only to surge again to a frightening number of new cases. With the continued shortage of nurses, Anna worked long hours, many times working double shifts, with very little sleep. Whenever possible, Dr. Morgan would whisk her away for a quick meal and a welcome change of scenery. Her days, and many times her nights, were filled with the needs of others. Their symptoms so familiar now as she learned to ease the ones she could and comfort the rest. And there was not one nurse who had been spared the experience of loss. Watching a patient, especially a child, lose their fight was nearly unbearable. And there had already been too many. There was little time, though, to dwell on anything for long.

Anna closed the door to her room quietly and was about to collapse onto the bed when she saw the envelope, with the unmistakable script, on her writing table. Her heart jumped into a rhythm she couldn't control. It beat with an excitement that rivaled her apprehension as she opened the letter.

My Dear Anna,

I know that your grandma has written you of all that has happened here. I wanted her to tell you about my sweet baby May. I am grateful to your grandma more than you can know. She is my connection to you. She may always be my only connection to you, and if that is true, I will understand. But she is wise, like my grandmother was, and she has been wanting me to write to you. I worried and decided that I shouldn't, but it weighs too heavy on my heart not to.

I write to tell you how sorry I am to have hurt you, even if you may never believe it. And I want to tell you why. I knew why even when I didn't want to know. Sometimes I believed that we could always be together. I could tell how much you wanted to believe it, too. But those times when we both knew how that could hurt us, I saw how you fought it. And each time you tried to find another way, and then I hoped again right along with you. But when Emily left, I felt your struggle. Your heart was tearing. Whatever you decided, the cost would be great. I thought I knew your heart. I thought you couldn't bring yourself to say what had to be said. So I made the only decision I could.

Was I wrong? Would you have chanced going North? Would you have left your Grandma alone, or stayed and dared being put in a mental hospital? What would you have decided? I ask now, too late. But the good that came of it is that you are where you should be. Without me, you have made a difference. You were there when so many needed you. With me, it would not have been possible.

I had dreams, too. Sometimes I still think of them, how I wanted to study and be a teacher or write powerful articles that would give girls courage to be more than they were told they could be. I would have been a good student. I want to learn so much. But your chance was much greater than mine, and it was only right that you take it. It lifts my spirits to hear Grandma Addy read how well you are doing. I am grateful to her for that, and for the papers she gives me to read. Reading the words of women like Miss Ida Wells, and reading about the bravery of Mary Church Terrell, gives me hope that my little one will have the chances that I didn't have. Maybe she will want to be a teacher or a nurse. Or maybe even a doctor or a scientist. I hope I will be able to say to her that she can be anything she wants to be, and it won't be just a dream.

Anna placed her hand over the letter on her lap, and moved it lightly over the words. A caress. Tears made their way down her cheeks. "Sweet Nessie," she whispered. "My sweet Nessie."

29

Anna smoothed back the dark wet hair from the forehead of the little boy in the last bed on the ward. He was finally falling off to sleep. The fever had broken; the aches that caused the whimpering and the restless movements were gone now. His arms and legs lay still and relaxed. She lingered long enough to watch the deep, even breaths, the last flicker of his eyelids, and to know that he was safely sleeping.

"You were worried about that little man, weren't you?" John met her in the doorway, speaking through the gauze mask covering his mouth and nose.

Anna nodded. "I sure was," she said through her own mask. "I kept the hot blanket packs on for only five minutes at a time, and followed them with cold compresses today, just as you said. I think you're right, it brings a high fever down faster than the method the other doctor is using. He's sleeping comfortably now."

"How about you?" he asked. "You look exhausted."

"Probably no more than you are."

They started down the lengthy hallway. "I'm worried about you," he said. "We've had another nurse go down sick today."

"Have they tried to get more volunteers from the churches? If we just had a couple more. Their taking care of bedding and pans, and bringing in fresh water, saves us a lot of time."

They dropped their masks in the waste container at the end of the hall. "I'll check with the administration in the morning," he said. "Meantime, you need to get a good night of sleep."

The routine had developed quite naturally, so that when they worked the same shift, John would walk her to the boarding house. She no longer noticed the slowness of his gait, but enjoyed the unhurried conversation and glimpses of normalcy as they walked: men coming home from work, women conversing on porch swings, and children chasing and playing and laughing. A tip of the scale, and much needed balance.

"There were fewer new cases today than yesterday," John said, "and fewer yesterday than the day before. We have to hope that this time the trend will hold."

"The Public Health Service is claiming that we have had fewer deaths than anywhere in the country."

"They're crediting that to their decision for strong preventative measures," he took her hand and squeezed it gently, "and to the dedication of so many fine nurses."

"You made that last part up," she replied, "or you would have included doctors."

He released her hand and smiled. "Such quickness. Now I see how you've become so accomplished in such a short time."

"You think so?"

"I do. That and the fact you're smart and quite passionate about your work. If there weren't such a shortage, I would fear for my position."

She looked at him directly and smiled. "That's a fine compliment, because you're a fine doctor. It is, of course, a fear you needn't have. I don't doubt that I could learn what is necessary, I doubt that I would have the opportunity to do it."

"You mustn't say that. There are women doctors coming out of Northern medical schools. If that is your dream . . . is it, Anna?"

"Going North once was."

"But you're here."

For reasons that she couldn't tell him. For a dream she would never expect him to understand. "I need to be closer in case my grandmother needs me."

He stopped on the last step of the porch as he always did. Tonight, though, he held her gaze instead of his usual goodnight kiss to her cheek.

"What is it?" Anna asked.

"I'm just struck by your compassion. I really shouldn't be, I see you with the children every day. But you gave up your dream."

She broke eye contact and searched for the right response. "It was complicated, John. I can't claim that it was a selfless decision. I don't think I can, anyway. I don't want you to think more highly of me than I deserve." That's what she saw in his eyes, an admiration undeserved, and she dared not explain why. Exactly the situation she had feared, and ignored. Shoved aside because she liked John. A good man, too good to be deceived. And yet, she had justified the time with him because it had been easy. Easy to learn from him, to talk and laugh with him, and easy to accept the feeling of respect that he offered.

"Have you ever felt privileged?" she asked.

John nodded. "I have," he said, "many times."

"Privileged in knowing that whatever your dream, if you want it badly enough and work hard enough, that it's really possible?"

"Hmm, I never thought about it like that. That it was a privilege."

"For a while, I didn't either. But it is, you know. For some . . . for some dreams. For others, though, a dream just means heartbreak."

His eyes didn't leave hers. She knew he would stand there, waiting, wanting to know more, for as long as she allowed. "I'm sorry," she said. "We're both tired, and I'm keeping you late and probably not making much sense."

"I've never met a woman like you," he said. "You question and wonder, and," he stopped and smiled, "make me think much too much. Do you think trying to figure you out is good for me?"

"No, I'm afraid it will be far too taxing. You should be saving your energy for your patients tomorrow."

He laughed, then leaned forward and kissed her cheek. "Sleep well tonight."

"Good night, John."

Sleeping well, or sleeping at all, would be a blessing. As tired as she was, Anna could not still the questions or calm her feelings. What was she to do with John? How close was too close? By all measure, she should be in love with him, anxious for their time together, tingling at his touch. Everything that she felt for Nessie she should be feeling for

John. But she didn't. And searching for why would only be wasted thought: it would not explain what she should do from here.

What would a good friend do? Wasn't she that, after all? No more, for sure, yet surely no less than a friend who cared deeply. He should know that, she should be sure that he knew. It would take the right amount of honesty, just enough and no more. She'd have to sort it out if she was going to avoid hurting him and free him to find a wife elsewhere. That was where this relationship was headed if she didn't do something now. Everything pointed toward the inevitable question—the way he watched her when he thought she didn't know, the exclusiveness, the conversations, of late, finding their way to financial plans and children. His hopes for the future.

But just as her mind was shifting through, finding some direction, the thought occurred to her that a life with John might be as good as she could expect. Would it be so bad, to know that she was loved, to have her opinions respected, to have no worry of acceptance? No fear of being committed, of being left in jail? Secrets would merely remain secrets. She would be Mrs. Morgan, married and free of societal scrutiny. Why not? She cared for John, enjoyed his company. Maybe one day she would even be able to say that she loved him, the way she was supposed to, the way a woman was supposed to love a man. Like Leda's husband, he would be supportive and respectful. How much would it matter that she felt no passion for him, no desire sparking and surging from his touch? Her life would be safe and secure—and gray. The brilliance that was hers and Nessie's, gone. The hope of ever having it again, gone as well.

What options were real? What in her heart was a fair choice? Accept the acceptable, bear children out of obligation, give only the part of herself that was left? Could she do that to John? Is it what Nessie did?

Anna reached for the light on the writing table and Nessie's letter. She propped herself on her elbow, and read it again. This time she heard the words, in the soft sweet voice that often disguised their power. But, not this time. "Whatever you decide, the cost would be great." The words shouted in their clarity. Nessie more than understood the consequences, she had faced them head on. Stood up and

". . . made the only decision that I could." The very thing that Anna couldn't do. Nessie hadn't given away their dream. She hadn't betrayed their love. She simply understood. She was still her Nessie, only braver and stronger than Anna had realized.

Anna finished the letter in tears. She wondered if lost dreams made Nessie cry, if she kept her tears until late at night and shed them when no one would know. If only it were possible to hold her then, to kiss the tears from her cheek, to whisper how much she wanted those dreams for her.

She wiped away her own tears before they could drop to the paper and mar Nessie's words. It was time. Past time, if she had listened to Grandma Addy. She needed to write to Nessie.

30

"Go back to the kitchen." The shout erupted from the side of the street, followed by "Women aren't smart enough to vote" and "Women will destroy this country."

Their message was clear, their intent to intimidate unmistakable. Leda's group of women, however, walking in the middle of the larger numbers of the Equal Suffrage Party, was undaunted.

Marches weren't new to Atlanta. Suffrage marches weren't new. Women, dressed in their best, had walked together side by side many times. Just like today, they had carried signs stating their message simply as "Votes for Women." And just like today, they had inspired support, and they had endured jeers.

New this time was the number of women marching and the numbers gathered in opposition. Silently they marched, hundreds of women, row after row, letting their presence and their signs speak for them.

The street was lined with people, two and three deep in some places, most watching out of curiosity. Some called out encouragement as women they knew passed by. The loudest voices, though, came from the opposition, louder and more determined now with the vote a real possibility. As the fear of federal legislation grew, so did membership in the Anti-Suffrage Organization. And they made themselves heard.

"Stealing pants won't make you a man." The jeers and misrepresentation continued as the march moved steadily down the street. At the rear was the only automobile, courtesy of The Men's Equal Suffrage League, carrying Adeline and two other women physically unable to march.

Millie Laughton sat confidently behind the wheel, driving her charges slowly behind the last row of marchers. "What do you think of your first automobile ride, Addy?" she asked.

"I'll be sure not to get too used to this, " she replied. "It sure is a bit easier on these old joints. You know, I never envisioned myself riding in an automobile."

Millie smiled.

Addy scanned a group of faces along the street, young faces, ones she didn't recognize. "It makes me think," she said, "that maybe I will get to vote before I die."

"It's going to happen, Addy. Every state that has given the vote on their own, has made it more apparent that those refusing should be forced by federal law."

"I need no more proof than this," Addy said, motioning to signs matching the jeers, "to know that that's what it will take for Georgia."

"I'll make you a promise, Addy. The day of the first election that we can legally vote, I will borrow this automobile again and personally drive you to the poll."

Addy smiled and nodded. "That's a promise I will hold you to."

Keeping the office open with all the commotion and distraction in town just wasn't good business sense. Thomas Benson Insurance was closed for the rest of the day, and many would say that valuable business hours were being sacrificed for a march of foolishness. More than foolish, if you were to ask Thomas. Dangerous, he would say, giving women power that they were ill equipped to handle. And knowing that his mother-in-law, and possibly his daughter, were demanding it, made his stomach roil.

He hadn't intended to go anywhere near the march. The sight of them, stiff-shouldered and sanctimonious, disrupting the entire city was more than he wanted to deal with today. Yet only minutes later, Thomas was maneuvering through the crowd, and scanning the faces as each row of marchers passed by, looking for Anna.

There were familiar faces, women who had made themselves

known in most unladylike ways. He felt for their families, he under-stood their embarrassment too well. What he did not understand were the men married to women like this. They allowed this debacle through their lack of control and self-respect. Weak-minded men, bowing to the whims of women. He had no sympathy for them, no use for them. He didn't see them in the men's club much anymore. Their defenses collapsed easily under rational argument. And The Men's Equal Suffrage League—well, they knew better than to offer anything more than private support. Lend a name, an automobile, but not a face. No, they knew better.

He worked his way through the crowd, closer to the street. Had he missed her? There were rows ahead of him, he could have missed her. Thomas squeezed between people and into the street, then hur-ried along the edge until he had checked each row. No Anna. Yes, he was sure. At least *she* didn't march. Adeline was another problem, one for which he had never found a solution. Unfortunately, too, one that he was sure to hear about at the club. They would say what he already knew: Women like Adeline were tainting the minds of younger women, tampering with the natural balance of the world. This small percentage of women would make everyone pay for their ignorance and self-importance. Coddling the Negroes, and now trying to destroy the integrity of elections—they had no idea the price.

Graham's was void of its normal lunch crowd. Anna and John, with their choice of tables, chose one at the window. By contrast, there was a bustle of activity outside as people made their way to the center of town.

John attended to seating Anna and took his seat across the table. "Were you able to see your grandmother?" he asked.

"Poor Gram," Anna replied. "We hardly had a chance to visit. She was so worried that Papa would see me."

"His weekly check-in with Mrs. Powell isn't enough to put his mind at ease?"

"Not on days like this," she said. "There was even something uneasy about Gram today. She's normally as sure and solid as an old oak. I've been able to count on that for as far back as I can remember. She's never waivered even face to face with Papa at his angriest. Do you think it's her age, that she feels vulnerable because she isn't as physically capable as she used to be?"

"We'll both have tea," John said to the woman waiting their table. He turned his attention back to Anna. "Try not to worry," he said. "It could just be the crowd: that's a lot of people. And, certainly not all of them friendly. That would test anyone's nerves."

She nodded, but Anna's mind was busy willing the sight of her grandmother. A vision of her sitting straight and tall, looking ahead, steadfast and confident. The way she always wanted her to be, the way she needed her to be.

John's voice interrupted her vision. "If it were up to you," he said, "you would be in the march instead of here, wouldn't you?"

"Not that the company isn't perfectly fine," she replied, "but, yes. It's not up to me, though. Very little is, these days."

He waited for her eyes to settle on his. "Let's go to the march then, together."

"Because you can protect me, stand up to my father for me, keep me from . . . ?" She stopped at the look on his face. No, she hadn't intended for it to sound like that. The words were intended, charging from thought to voice before she could change her mind. But, the tone, chilled and sharp, would have been better aimed at her father.

"I don't understand. I thought that was what you wanted."

Of course he would think that. Why wouldn't he? "I'm sorry, John. I know that that was from your heart, and I do appreciate it." His frown lingered. "I don't know if I can explain how I feel."

"Try, Anna. I do want to understand."

"Even if it contradicts much of what you assume is right?"

"Yes." The waitress appeared for their order. "Give us a few minutes," John said.

A few minutes, Anna thought. Not even a few hours would help. A lifetime, it would take a lifetime to explain it. It had taken her this long, after all. He was waiting, expecting her to make it clear, to help him understand. And she wanted to, if she could only find the words, the right ones, to define what she knew now.

"I don't want to offend you," she began. "You're a good man, and you've become a good friend. This is about me, not you."

"Then why would I be offended?"

Precisely why, she would never tell him. That part of her, no one except Nessie would ever know. It was their last secret. And it had nothing to do with the value of her thought or her worth as a woman. What he did need to know, though, had everything to do with it, with her freedom, with her sense of who she knew she was. He needed to know what compromises she could no longer weigh, what were no longer options in her life.

The waitress, impatient for their order, had returned. "Anna, how does the chicken cobbler sound today?" John asked.

"That's fine," she replied.

"Then, make that two," he told the waitress. As she retreated to the kitchen, John redirected his attention to Anna. "So what don't I know about Grady's prettiest nurse?"

"I wouldn't mind ordering for myself," she said, and noted the playful rise of his eyebrows. Yes, she thought, that one wasn't so bad. "That's only part of a bigger issue, though."

"Which is?"

"Independence." No turning back now. "I want to decide what is best for me. I want to choose my own friends, speak my mind, take risks. I want to make my own money and not depend on a man to take care of me."

It might have been too much, too quickly, but once she began she dared not stop for fear that her chance would be over. An irrational fear maybe, with John, but there had been so few other chances, and she would not lose this one.

She tried to read his expression, but it told her nothing. He seemed to be assessing, maybe wondering how what he had heard would affect him. He was calm, unemotional, so unlike Papa.

His eyes remained on hers. "You're wrong," he said.

Anna offered only a frown.

"Not about what you want," he continued. "About it not being about me. Or, at least, what is expected of me. Would you fault me for trying to keep you safe, or for wanting to provide a good home for you?"

"I would fault you for doubting my ability, or denying me opportunity," she said, her eyes steady on his.

"Well, then," he began, offering a relief of a smile, "you would find no reason to fault me."

"And what would you do with the criticism, the inevitable embarrassment you'll feel when people shun me or mock me, or you for allowing such behavior from your woman? Would you try to hide it from me, from others?"

Their meals had been served without either of them acknowledging it. There was no quick response from John, and no smile. The lack of movement and conversation in the restaurant amplified the silence between them. Anna waited, nearly sure that she had said too much, and feigned interest in her cobbler.

"I don't know how to answer that," he said.

"You don't have to."

"No. I do. I want to, but it's not a simple answer. It rarely is with you."

"I'm sorry, John. I didn't intend to ruin our lunch."

"You haven't at all," he said. "You've challenged me, again, to step into someone else's life and see the world as they see it . . . *your* life this time, something I thought I understood."

"It's perfectly fine to enjoy your lunch while it's warm, and worry about sorting out my life later."

John finally smiled. "Well, I know two things without further thought. You would not embarrass me, and I would not ask your father for your hand. That would be your decision entirely."

Anna had known for some time what a special man, what a special person, John was. Today, though, she had learned something about herself. She could look beyond what would make her life easier. She could sacrifice a settled, comfortable, respected life because of how much she cared for this man. Yes, she would.

"Well, I have two things that I need to tell *you*," she began. "I *would* embarrass you, either by my actions, or by how others would react to them. You're the kind of man, though, who would hide it well, and remain supportive. I know that." Easy enough to hear. His eyes confirmed it. He knew what they were saying about the Suffragettes;

186

it wouldn't be hard to personalize it. The rest of what she had to say, however, wouldn't be so easy for him to hear.

"The other thing I want you to know truly is only about me. You need to know that if I were to ever marry, I know that I could never find a better man than you. But there is a fight in me, and an anger of sorts, that won't allow it. To marry, knowing that I couldn't devote one hundred percent of myself would be unfair to you. You deserve so much better, John."

There it was, there in his eyes, exactly what she had dreaded. She knew it would hurt him. But, knowing didn't make it any easier to see it. His eyes held hers with a gentle plea.

"Anna, I would never ask for more than you could give."

Her gaze softened, the sharpness of her purpose gone. "And for now, maybe for a while, that will be enough for you. But someday it won't be."

His voice struggled to lift, his eyes offered the last of his hope. "You say this now, but maybe in time . . ."

"I know what you want your life to be, you've told me about your dreams and what would make you happy. I will not be the one to keep you from those dreams."

"How can you be so sure that you would? Anna—"

"I'm sure of one thing, that you would sacrifice what you really want if you thought it would make me happy. And I care for you too much to let that happen."

Whether it was what he heard in her voice or what he saw in her face, John's expression seemed to settle into a resolve. He lowered his gaze for a moment, then reached across the table to take her hand. His eyes came back to hers. "So what does this mean, for us, for our friendship?"

"That has to be your decision."

"I've had childhood friends," he began, "friends that I made in medical school, and colleagues that I consider friends. But I have never met anyone like you. I don't want to lose you from my life."

"You're a special person, John. I worried that if we didn't marry I would lose your friendship. And I realize that when you do marry, our friendship may have to change, but I don't want to lose it."

187

"I can't promise that I will ever stop wishing that you could be my wife," he said, gently squeezing her hand, "but I can promise that you will always have my friendship."

31

The sun had begun its descent, leaving a bright pink backdrop silhouetting the frame of the big house and making a filigree of the branches of the giant tree. Nessie moved swiftly along the path, with Rufus close on her heels, his long strides alternating from one side of her to the other.

"What's you gotta be coming up here tonight for?" he asked, the smell of alcohol coating his words.

"I told you," Nessie replied. "I promised to help Grandma Addy put up the rest of the tomatoes. Go on home, Rufus."

"You," he began, then tripped against Nessie's heel and nearly fell. "You shouldn't be comin' home after dark."

"I've been walkin' this path day and night since I could walk. Now, go on home."

After a few more steps with Rufus still following, Nessie stopped and turned around. He smiled that smile, that big silly toothy smile, and leaned forward to wrap his arms around her. "I gotta take care o' my girl."

"You had too much to drink to be takin' care of *yourself*," she said, wriggling free of his arms. "Go on, now. See if Momma needs help getting' May to sleep. Sing her the butterfly song."

"Flutter along, sweet May, sweet May," he sang, "off to sleep on butterfly wings . . ."

Nessie grasped his arms and turned him around. "Go," she said.

"Sweet May, sweet May," he sang, starting down the path toward home.

Nessie shook her head and smiled. She couldn't help it. As much as he frustrated her at times, many times, he still had a way of making her smile. No matter how well meant his intent, though, she would not let him spoil her special time with Grandma Addy. He would never be able to understand, even if it were something she could tell him.

Nessie hurried up the back steps with a sense of relief, and hopeful for a new letter from Anna.

"Thank you, Nessie," Addy said from her seat on the kitchen stool. "Your momma and I filled half the jars, but it's been a long day. It's so good of you to help me. We'll just get these finished up tonight and get the other half tomorrow. I don't want to keep you from your little one too long."

"I don't mind. Little May'll be just fine. I sent Rufus on home to sing her to sleep. He needs something more important than following after me tonight. He gets a certain amount of alcohol in him, and all he wants to do is hang on to me wherever I am."

"You just have to look at the blessings he brings," Addy said.

Nessie smiled, sliding the handle of a wooden spoon up and down inside the edge of a filled jar to free the air bubbles. "He's surely been a blessing to Papa. His chin was bumpin' on his knees when Coca Cola cut his shift, but Papa's been countin' on him to do the work he can't do now. He don't quit every day 'til it's done. Gives Papa a lot o' relief."

"I know your Papa was nervous about the new plan, but it's working. Livestock sales have brought in a good profit for both of us. We're both feeling a bit of relief lately. A fine feeling," she said with a nod to Nessie. "You get the air out of those jars while I get the rings and lids on. Then check to see if the water is ready."

They worked well together, and before long Nessie was placing the jars in the two big canners on the stove.

"We'll let them boil for about forty-five minutes," Addy said, easing down from the stool. "While you get those in there, I'll see if these old joints'll let me check the mail Mr. Shakly put in the parlor. Maybe there's a special letter to read."

Her first few steps were stiff, locking her into a painful stoop. By the time Addy reached the hall, she had managed to straighten her posture enough to lessen the pain. Keeping moving was a must: she would not be bedridden. This was a promise Addy had made to herself; she would not go easy from this world.

She heard the sounds first, voices outside the front of the house, as she entered the room. There was movement, then a streak of light, beyond the sheer of the drapes. Addy moved to the window and reached to separate the drapes when a whoosh of orange lit up the yard and the parlor.

Startled, she stepped back from the window and had to catch her balance by grabbing the arm of the love seat. The form was clear now, a fiery cross blazing a glow over horses and hooded figures.

Heart pounding hard and fear driving old legs faster than should have been possible, Addy burst into the doorway of the kitchen. "Nessie, don't ask questions, just hand me the gun behind the door."

Nessie jumped quickly into action, grabbed the rifle, and rushed it to Addy.

Her eyes, wide and intense, told Addy that she understood all that was necessary. "Run," Addy said, "as fast as you can get home. Go!"

Nessie was out the door in an instant and Addy hurried to the front door. Adrenaline racing, she was ready. She would face them, let them know that she was not intimidated, stand strong. The message, delivered in a booming voice, penetrated the door, "No petticoat rule, and no nigger lovers." It set Addy's jaw into a hard line and steeled her will, but what she saw when she flung open the door nearly buckled her knees.

Her yell, "Noooo," erupted as she hoisted the rifle and fired over their heads. This confrontation, by an old woman and a gun, was unexpected, and caused the nearest horse to rear in fright, and dump its hooded rider. The horse, in its panic, trampled the fallen rider. Someone grabbed the wounded man and helped him onto the wagon, as the rest headed toward the road. Addy rushed from the porch to the tree, grabbed the thin, dangling legs, wrapped her arms tightly around them, and lifted.

"Dear God, no," she cried. "Please, no!"

The unmistakable sound of a gunshot carried over the field, causing Jackson to drop the armful of firewood and run to the front of the house. The sky glowed orange over the roof of the big house.

"Papa," he yelled as he burst through the front door.

"I heard," he said.

"There's fire at Miss Adeline's."

"Nessie," Willa said. "Nessie's there."

"Jackson, get Rufus and the rifles. Get goin'. I'll follow on the mule."

"Rufus went with Nessie," he replied.

There was nothing else said, it wasn't necessary. Jackson bolted out the door. Calvin hobbled as fast as he could move to the barn.

As he neared the beginning of the path, Jackson heard someone approaching. The moon, shrouded in clouds, offered no help until he was closer and could make out the outline of his sister.

"Nessie," he called, "you and Rufus okay?"

Breathless, Nessie grabbed Jackson's arm. "I sent him home . . . Jackson, where is he?"

"Stay here," he said, entering the path and quickly hitting full stride.

On legs shaking with surges of adrenaline, Nessie turned and followed him. His urgency, and the thought that Rufus had not gone home, drove her legs as hard now as the gunshot had driven them in retreat.

Addy held him longer than she should have been able to, her arms tight around his legs, her head pressed against his thigh. "Please," Addy cried, fighting off sobs that threatened what strength she had left.

The movements she had felt when she first grabbed him, the struggle in his legs, had stopped. "No, Rufus, no." Addy pushed up again, trying to hold him higher. Was he moving again, or was it the quivering of her own muscles? It didn't matter; she would hold him as long as her body would let her. If she could will the strength—send it from her mind to her muscles—if only she could. Her mind so much stronger, her body so tired.

Jackson rounded the back corner of the big house cautiously, rifle ready. What he saw made him drop the gun, run to the tree, and scramble up to the limb to release the rope.

The sudden release dropped Rufus's full weight, and took Addy to the ground. He was limp, and heavy for such a thin frame. Addy crawled to his side. Jackson was frantically removing the rope from around his neck. Addy cradled his head with her arm, and in that moment when she looked into the stare of his eyes, she saw her Billy there. Felt the heaviness, the fragility, of her Billy once again right there under the tree. Tears streamed down her cheeks, for Billy, for Rufus.

She'd have to find a way, once again, to take a weight from her heart, but how could she answer the soft cries next to her?

Nessie leaned close, her head settling against the side of Addy's. "Oh, Rufus. My sweet, Rufus." Her tears wet his cheeks, and she gently brushed them away. "Is he gone?" she cried. "Oh, nooo, he's gone." She brought her eyes to meet Addy's. "He's gone, isn't he?"

Seeing all the sorrow in Nessie's eyes, Addy knew that if her own heart could hold it all, all the pain, then it would, she would take it—all of it. Addy gathered Nessie to her, nestled her face against her shoulder, and whispered softly, "I'm sorry, sweet girl, I'm so sorry."

Jackson couldn't stand still, pacing from the corner of the house and back, around the women, and back again. He said nothing, only paced, until his father arrived, slid from the mule, and knelt beside Nessie. He put his hand on Rufus's chest and held his cheek close to his nose. When he was sure, he raised his eyes to Addy's, and embraced his daughter.

"Lewis was right," Jackson blurted against the silence. "It don't matter. It don't matter what we do."

Calvin helped Nessie to her feet, and directed his words at Jackson. "Take your sister home, and then bring the wagon."

Addy lowered Rufus's head gently to the ground. "It was because of me," she said, as Calvin began to help her up. "They're angry at me." She was grateful for his strength, letting him lift her, first to her knees, and then to her feet. Her body had used what little reserve it had. Her legs barely held her weight. "I have to call the police," she said, leaning heavily on Calvin as they made their way to the house. "Rufus never hurt anyone."

"You do what you think you must," Calvin said, "but you and I know nothing will come of it. Just as Jackson said, it doesn't matter. There's nothing to be done—but grieve."

32

Anna checked the last of her young patients. The little blonde head lifted from the pillow. Her voice seemed so small in the bigness of the room around her. "Nurse Anna?"

"Yes, Sweetie."

"It's okay if you have to go home," she said, clutching the doll Anna had made for her. "Miss Annabelle will keep me company until you come back."

"And that's exactly what she is supposed to do," Anna replied. "I'll be back before you know it." She pulled the blanket up over the little girl's shoulder and returned the smile.

Today had been a good day, no fatalities and more children on the mend. Now that she thought about it, the whole week had been a good one. Better than any she could remember in a long time. Admissions of new flu cases were at the lowest since the outbreak. She had been as honest as she had dared with John, and still had his friendship. There had been time and enough energy to finish two dolls for her patients, and she had written the long-avoided letter to Nessie. So much of the stress that had weighed both her days and nights was gone.

She felt light, as if a gentle breeze could gather beneath her skirt and carry her down the hall. Tonight would be a night of relief, a night for her, tucked into her nightclothes early and savoring hot tea and lemon and a good book. She would immerse herself in the world of *The Lamp in the Desert*, and find out how Stella traveled to India unescorted, and overcame ostracism and deception to find love. Then she would decide for herself if that were really possible.

The thoughts quickened her descent of the wide cement steps and

195

made her smile. But John's voice, calling out from the doorway, stopped her near the bottom.

"Anna, I'm so glad I caught you," he said, moving as quickly as he could down the steps. "It's your father."

"My *father*?"

"A colleague at Piedmont just let me know that he was admitted into emergency. Come on, I'll take you."

He was clearly in distress, arms clutched around his middle, and grimacing in pain. Anna stood beside her father's bed while John spoke with the doctor on call.

"Papa, what happened?"

He turned his head toward his daughter. "Anna," he said and reached for her hand. He shortened a breath with a wince, but managed, "Nothing to worry over."

"Are you sick? Did someone hurt you?"

"An accident," John said, joining her at the bedside. "A spooked horse. Most likely some broken ribs."

"Have they given him something for the pain?" she asked.

John nodded. "Give it a little more time to ease the muscle spasms."

"You don't worry, Anna." Her father offered a feeble smile. "They're taking good care of me here."

Here. Not the Grady's, where public money and Negro admittance surely mean less than adequate care. She was still doing it, reading the negative in everything he said. *Even now, when he's vulnerable and in pain, and may not have meant to insinuate that at all.* She shook the thought, and looked at her father. "I'm going to stay until I'm sure that you're going to be all right."

"I'll stay with you," John said, "and see you home."

Thomas squeezed Anna's hand. "The best medicine for me," he offered with another attempt at a smile, "is a good man taking care of my daughter."

Another thought to shake.

There had been a fleeting hope, as Anna dressed for the day, that today she would enjoy the relief she had looked forward to last night. But the message waiting for her at breakfast dashed that hope. Mr. Shakly was on his way to pick her up and take her home.

He was there before Anna had much time to worry, and she was grateful to the years of loyalty that allowed him to tell her exactly what had happened. The tears that followed were for Nessie, for Rufus; the agitation shaking her body was for the fight boiling in her gut. The fight that needed only the sight of the charred cross in the yard to heat it over the edge.

She jumped from the buggy the second it stopped and rushed to the house. Her first and most urgent concern was that her grandmother was still in bed. Anna entered the bedroom on a rush of air, and with obvious concern coloring her face.

"Gram, oh, Gram." Anna leaned over and embraced her grandmother. Her first reassurance came from Addy's arms wrapping firmly around her back. "Are you all right? What can I do?"

"Help me get out of this bed. These old bones took all they could last night." Addy kept her firm grip around Anna and let her pull her up to sit on the edge of the bed.

"I should have known something would happen. All the hate," Anna said. "I should have been here."

"No, Anna." She grasped Anna's head with both hands and looked directly into her eyes. "No."

Anna backed up a step and gave her grandmother room to massage the muscles of her thighs. Her muscles might be weak, her body tired, but Addy's will was as strong as steel. Respect it, she would. But Anna had found a will of her own.

"I know," Anna began, "that until the day that you die, you will do everything you can to protect me. I know that. I love that about you. But don't you know what you've given me? The self-worth to know who I am, the strength to stand against anyone who would deny me that worth. I learned that from you. And I've learned how difficult the battle is. "She locked her eyes firmly on Addy's. "No

197

matter how hard the fight, they will pay for this, Gram. They will pay."

"It's a dangerous battle," Addy replied.

"Would you have lived your life any other way? Would you have chosen compromise, not to fight for what you believe?"

"People have died because of me, before," Addy said, "and now."

"You," Anna said, looking into the pale blue eyes, "did not kill them. Someone else made that decision. That's on *their* soul, not yours."

"You don't know all of it, Anna."

"I know that no matter how long I live, or how hard the battle, no one will ever take away what you've given me."

"There's something you must know, then," Addy said, motioning for Anna to sit next to her. "If part of the battle you face is another one I know well, then I need to tell you about my Billy."

Anna reached her arm around her grandmother and pulled her close. "I know what happened, Gram. About the Captain and everything. It's still a secret, no one will know."

"No, you don't know it all. There's something no one else knows," she said, facing her granddaughter. "Anna, Billy was a woman."

The surprise caught her breath, sent a zing, an inaudible, unexpressed shot straight to her heart. She searched the familiar eyes, waiting for something—a change, something different. But there was no change in them, just the same directness, the same honesty—waiting for her, expecting the same in return. Her thoughts raced back over what Nessie had told her, re-linking what she thought she had known. And, then, "Did the Captain know?"

"No," Addy replied. "He killed Billy because he thought she was a man."

The questions were forming faster than Anna could ask them. "What if he had known?"

Addy broke eye contact and let her gaze drift. "My worry then was for Billy, my strong-willed, noble Billy, fighting for the North. I was right to worry."

"Had you ever thought past the war, if Billy had come back after, and the Captain?"

"I imagined going North with her. She had moved her mother there for safety."

198

"The Captain would have committed you, wouldn't he, if he had known?"

Addy's eyes came back. "You understand the danger, don't you? That it continues?"

Anna nodded.

"I know your heart, Anna. I think I have always known your heart." She pushed against the edge of the bed, leaning forward as Anna helped her to her feet. She straightened slowly, and turned to touch her hand to Anna's cheek. "Go to Nessie."

Jackson answered the door. Tall and broad shouldered, a young man now, politely ushering her in. Low lamplight and quiet voices showed respect for Rufus lying in an open wooden coffin on the far side of the room.

Anna met Nessie's eyes, dark and sad, and lovely. It felt as though something clutched her heart and squeezed it so tightly that she couldn't breathe. She wasn't prepared for the mire of emotions. Hurt and forgiveness struggled against love, and the only one she could safely allow its expression was sadness. She acknowledged it in each of their faces, then paid her respects to Rufus.

The body lying there was not Rufus at all, she decided. There was no twinkle of mischief defining his eyes, no wide boyish smile to warm the coldest of hearts. And no sense of peace—that relaxation of anguish like she had seen on her mother's face, the indication to those left behind that he was indeed in a better place. No, she didn't see that. She felt only her sense of loss, of senseless loss and vacancy. And, past that, anger.

Anna sat with the family, listened to their grief and shared their sadness. She listened as they told her all they could about what had happened. She would have understood blame, had they directed it at the meetings, and the agitation they must have caused, or at her grandmother. There was none. No blame, no expectation of justice. Only grief and an unnerving acceptance that she could not understand.

"The gunshot." She directed her concern to Calvin. "Do you know if my grandmother shot any of them?"

"I wondered that," he replied. "I worried about what would come after if she did. But she said she shot in the air. The worse that happened was spookin' a horse and it throwin' the rider. Don't think they'd be back on that. We got to hope anyway."

"I'm staying with her tonight. I'll be watchful."

"Your grandmother did all she could," Calvin said as Anna stood to leave. "Holdin' him like that for so long. There was nothin' else she could do. You tell her that."

"I will."

Nessie walked her out and closed the door behind them. In an instant she was in Anna's arms, holding her tightly, tears wetting the curve of Anna's neck.

The mire of emotion was gone. No thought, nor worry, nor question. Only the feel of Nessie in her arms. Only love. Anna tightened her arms, and pressed her cheek against Nessie's head.

"I'll bring Gram to the funeral," Anna whispered. "She wants to be there."

"Will you meet me after?" Nessie asked.

"Yes."

The sound of the door loosened their embrace and separated them.

"I'll walk you back," Jackson said. "Just in case."

33

At the time, Calvin's answer had served as relief, her grandmother shooting in the air and maybe averting further danger. As Anna had walked the path home, though, Jackson silent at her side, the information fit itself into a larger picture. When she saw it, understood its implications, anger reached a level she had never known. There would be no sleep that night, only a constant attempt at containment. A harnessing of an anger that continued to bubble up from a depth that spanned years. The dismissiveness, the disrespect, the blatant unfairness—all those times she had watched it, and felt it, and endured it, melting together and roiling to an unbearable heat. She had to control it, find a way to use it. Such a power. Surely she could find a way to use it. And if she could control that kind of power, what else could she control?

Early in the morning, once she knew her grandmother was up and moving well enough, Anna took the buggy into town alone. Her first stop was at Grady to give an explanation for needing a leave from her shift, and to ask a favor of John. He provided exactly what she wanted. It hadn't taken long for him to find that there had been only one patient suffering from a horse accident admitted to any of the hospitals last night. It was all she needed.

He wasn't surprised to see her. It was expected, after all, for a daughter to show her concern, for her to check on her father's healing. Proper. Yes, it would be the proper thing to do.

Her visit, though, had nothing to do with "proper." Anna pulled the curtain closed that separated her father's bed from the rest of the room. He smiled and reached for her. She refused him both her smile and her hand.

"How is your pain?" she asked.

"Tolerable. With the pain medication, it's tolerable."

She struggled to control her anger, to keep it contained and measure its doses. If she freed it, allowed it to reign, she would place her hands on his chest and make him feel the full weight of it. She would cause him pain beyond tolerance, beyond medication, beyond his next breath. She struggled with the temptation.

"A horse accident, the doctor said. Something spooked it, and it threw you?"

"Yes," he replied, "an unfortunate accident."

"What was it that spooked the horse?"

"Oh," he said with a weak shake of his head, "it happened so fast. Not worth talking about. Tell me about your young man, the doctor."

"No." She spat the words, firm and low. "You're going to listen to what I have to say."

"You will not speak to me in that tone."

There was no power left in his words. Nothing that would stop the game of chance that she was determined to play, and to win. "I will speak to you however I wish." She watched his face, waiting for his anger. "I haven't one shred of respect left for you that would stop me."

There it was. His eyes narrowed on hers. He tried to push himself up to face her, but collapsed to the pillow in pain.

Anna leaned closer over the bed. Her voice was low, her eyes bore into his. "You see, I know what spooked that horse. I know where you were, and I know what you did."

"You don't know anything."

"There was one thing I didn't know." She straightened her posture. "Whether you would own your actions. As despicable as they are. If you would claim your convictions, or if you would hide them like a coward. True character marches openly. Cowards wear hoods."

His voice rose to as high as the next spasm would allow. "Get out of here. You are an embarrassment."

"What you think of me doesn't matter anymore. It used to, when I was a child and I longed for your approval and your love." She leaned over him again. "But now, I loathe you. And there's nothing you will ever be able to do to change that."

He tried to lock her in an intimidating glare. "I'll put you where embarrassments belong."

"Commit me?" She returned his glare, steeled herself to turn the last of her cards, the ace she was counting on. Threatening to turn in what she suspected he had done, no, what she *knew* he had done, to the police would be a bluff. He knew that. No Klan member will have to pay the price. But this, *this* card was no bluff. What justice could, or would, not do, she would. In a society that values reputation over justice, you throw your ace and take control over your life. "Before you make that move, you should think about how your business and social friends will feel when they're told that you grew your company by stealing wealthy clients from Thacker & Son."

The reaction she saw was exactly what she had hoped for. He was surprised, shocked probably, and angry. "I've never—"

"No? I wonder if they will believe that. I wonder how you will convince them."

"It's a lie. It would . . ."

"Destroy you? Your precious business, your reputation, the hallowed place in society that you cherished more than your wife, or your children? Would it destroy all that?"

She could tell that he was grasping for control. His face blanched, his eyes widened. "They would never believe the, the *ramblings* of a woman like you."

Anna frowned. "Probably not," she said and lowered her eyes. She feigned a turn to leave, then looked at him once more. "That's why they won't hear it from me."

There were so many things that Nessie wanted to say, really needed to say. She thought about how to say them on the walk to the little house. Her biggest worry was that she no longer knew who Anna was. How much had she changed? Could she still feel the love she once had for Nessie, despite the hurt Nessie had caused her? Part of her was terrified to find out. So much had happened, so many feelings to sort out. But a bigger part of her had to know.

All of it, though, the worry, the uncertainty, vanished the moment she saw Anna. She was sitting on the cot, still in her black skirt and blouse, the box of letters on her lap.

The tears, evident when Anna lifted her head, sent Nessie to her side. Anna grabbed her in a tight embrace. "I'm so sorry about Rufus. Oh, Nessie, I'm sorry."

It was easy with Anna, to give in to the sadness, to give herself the time to truly grieve, to cry. With all the chaos and fear, and things needing to be done, there hadn't been the quiet time, the space to give in. They cried together for as long as Nessie needed, until the words came easy.

"He had a huge heart, Anna." Nessie wiped the tears from her face with the palm of her hands. "He never had a harsh word for anyone."

Anna nodded, dried her own tears with the sleeve of her blouse. "I loved his smile and his good spirit."

Nessie managed a smile. "May'd a been playin' tricks on me with her papa before long." Just as important as the time to cry, was the time to talk. And Anna was listening. Nessie placed her hand over her abdomen. "He'll never get to see his new baby."

Anna's eyes widened. She smiled and placed her hand over Nessie's. "Have you told your momma?"

"Not yet. I was just sure this week . . . Rufus knew." Nessie picked up the box of letters wedged between them. "Did you read them all?"

"I hope it was all right. I hadn't been back here since . . ." She dropped her eyes away from Nessie. "But, the minute I walked in, everything was exactly the same. It smelled just as I remembered, and it felt like our place again where we shared all our secrets and dreams. I don't know what made me look in the hiding place."

"I didn't think you'd ever see them. I couldn't keep it all inside me. I had to get it out, so I wrote them like I was talkin' to you. But I couldn't send them."

"The same way I couldn't write you for so long," Anna said.

"You wrote me?"

"Gram kept telling me to write you, but I was too hurt."

"I knew I hurt you. I told her you didn't want to hear from me. Why did you finally do it?"

"I saw things that made me realize how selfish I was. How headstrong and unaware. I thought we could make things happen the way we wanted them to. I didn't see the risks or understand the danger. You did, Ness. And you knew there was only one way you could make me see it. I know that now. There are a lot of things that I can't make happen the way *I* want them, and I can't assume that if they *were* possible that they would be right for you."

"But you know what has always been in my heart, you read it," Nessie said, fingering the letters. "I couldn't say it out loud then. If I had, you never would have gone. But, you know it now, you know I could never love anyone like I love you."

Anna nodded and pulled Nessie into an embrace. "There was something else that I realized," she said softly. "I would go on alone if I didn't have your love."

Nessie settled in against her and welcomed the special heat that always happened between them. "What are we going to do?"

"Grieve, and search our hearts, and I'll trust that what you decide is right."

"The one thing I know for sure. As bad as my heart hurts, you make it want to keep beatin'. I just want to stay right here." This was the solace that mattered most, more than her mother's arms or her father's strength, it was the place where her heart was home. There was nowhere else she could lay her heart bare and know it was safe.

"There's something I need to tell you," Anna said, waiting until Nessie lifted her head. "I'm not sure that this is the right time, but you have to know."

"As long as I know you love me, you can tell me anything."

"I love you more than anything, Nessie." She frowned and hesitated for a moment before saying, "My father was one of the Klansmen."

Nessie sat up from their embrace. "You're sure? Your father?"

"Sure enough to threaten him. If he doesn't leave us alone, I'll start a rumor he'll never live down."

"Does your grandmother know?"

"I'll tell her tonight. I don't think it will be a shock to her."

34

May found the unfinished doll in the sewing basket before Nessie swooped in and grabbed up the basket.

"It's been a very long time," Addy said, "since I've had to worry about keeping things out of a baby's reach. Anna, you'd better check around the room here."

Smiling with excitement, May waived the doll in the air, lost her balance, and sat down hard on her butt.

"Oh," Anna exclaimed, reaching for the toddler.

Nessie laughed. "She's fine. Most times she just laughs. Got her momma's rough and tumble genes."

So the parlor was swept clear of danger, and May set about to explore and entertain. Her antics and miscues narrowed the world to a small bundle of innocence. For a while their little world knew nothing of hatred or injustice, only joy and laughter, contagious and therapeutic.

It was a slower trip across the floor this time. May headed once again for Anna sitting on the love seat with Nessie. She grabbed a fistful of Anna's skirt, and then another, and pulled herself up to lay her head on Anna's leg.

"I think our little entertainer is done in for the night," Addy said.

Anna picked up a sleepy May, and cradled her on her lap, where she snuggled against Anna's breast and closed her eyes.

"Yes," Addy said, slowly rising from the rocker, "she has the right idea. I'm going to turn in, too." As she passed the girls, she added, "You know where the rifle is."

"Try not to worry, Gram. We all need a good night's sleep."

May stirred, but didn't wake. Anna leaned down and kissed her head. "She's a sweet one, Nessie."

There was nothing more beautiful, Nessie decided. The golden glow of the lamp warming the tones of Anna's face, honey-brown hair falling over her shoulder, her gaze laying gently over little May in her arms.

Nessie reached up and touched Anna's face, and waited for her eyes. "I wish this was possible for us."

"Maybe it is," Anna said softly. "There's something I've been waiting to tell you."

"If the world hasn't changed," Nessie said, withdrawing her hand, "Wishin's all we got."

"Something *has* changed, at least knowing about it has. Gram knows all too well how hard it is for me to hold my tongue." She raised her eyebrows. "And you know. I can't even count how many times she's schooled me about it. She tried hard to teach me temperance." Anna nodded at Nessie's smile. "Well, you both would have been proud of how I handled my anger, my *severe* anger, at my father. I worried her enough the other night, though, for her to tell me the rest of the secret."

Nessie thought for a moment. "Billy?"

Anna nodded. "Nessie," she said, looking into the anxious eyes that she had missed so much, "Billy was a woman."

It wasn't really a surprise. It just made sense, perfect sense, Nessie thought. The protectiveness, the understanding, looking the other way when there was so much opposition to even a friendship. "That's why," she said, "we were allowed to be for so long."

"It explains a lot," Anna replied. "Why I thought that everyone would naturally treat us the same way. I see now how much she struggled with that."

"She tried to protect you *and* your heart, even after what happened to Billy. And she's given us something she never had: someone who understands."

"Maybe there is something possible for us, Nessie. I'm going to move out of the boarding house and come back here. I've already decided. I'll take the buggy in to the hospital every day myself. They can say what they will. I'm not afraid of my father anymore, and I won't leave Gram alone any longer." She searched Nessie's face for a hint that she saw the same possibility, but she found nothing. "Could this be a place for us?"

"You're not going to like this. I know you won't. There's only one way this could be a place for us, and that's if I am working here. Only if everyone knows I'd be takin' the place of my mother."

Anna pleaded softly. "No, Nessie."

"You told me that just because it was possible you wouldn't assume it was the right thing for me."

Anna tilted her head. "It's easier to say than to do. I'm not good at this, you know I'm not."

My Anna, Nessie thought. *Still my stubborn dreamer.* "What happened to Rufus can happen again, no matter where we are. We got no protection. We can't change it. You have to trust me. There's only one way we can be together. Everyone has to believe I only work for you."

The baby stretched her legs and repositioned herself.

"Your arm's falling asleep, isn't it?" Nessie asked. She leaned over, slipped her arms under May and pulled her over onto her lap. "She's a grain bag when she's sleepin'."

Anna moved her arm around to restore the circulation. "What about your dreams, Ness?" Anna took Nessie's face in her hands. "Please don't give up on your dreams."

Nessie leaned forward and kissed her. Warm and tender touches, she pressed her lips to Anna's, told her that she loved her, told her it was okay. And when she left their kiss and pressed her forehead to Anna's lips, she said, "Bring me books." She lifted her face, curled the corners of her mouth. "I'll read everything."

Anna smiled.

"I'm going to write essays, like Miss Wells. I've thought about it for a while. I'll have a pen name."

"And we'll send them to publications all over the country," Anna added. "We won't settle, Ness, it will only look like we have."

"I got a lot inside me that needs sayin'. I can write it better than I can say it."

"You say it just fine."

"I might not ever get to go to college, but—" Nessie looked down at May in her arms "—I'm gonna do all I can to be sure my baby can."

"I can't think of a more important mission."

EPILOGUE

May 1919

Leda's voice at the other end of the phone line was crackling with excitement. "The vote was 24 to 1, Addy. They passed it. In some ways it's a small step, it's just the municipal primary. But Addy . . . we're going to vote."

The feeling was indescribable, because it was just that, a feeling. A sense that the world had shifted beneath her, and she was standing in a different place. Addy tried calling Anna into the room with a somewhat frightening urgency. The words trembled uncharacteristically, but their message was a powerful one.

Anna leaned over the rocker and wrapped her arms around her grandmother. She pressed her face against the softly wrinkled cheek. "It's happening, Gram. It's really happening."

The promise was kept. Millie Laughton borrowed the automobile, just as she said she would, and drove Addy to the poll.

"Your voice, Addy," she said, "and mine and Anna's, and every one of these women gets counted today."

The line of women had begun forming early, standing politely, patiently, along the walk, waiting for the poll to open. A handful of men, regular voters, milled around the front of the building. They talked among themselves between insulting comments they directed at the line of women. Their numbers would grow over the course of the day and so would their protest. It was to be expected.

Yet the women were undaunted. Many reached a hand out to her as Addy moved slowly toward Leda, waiting for her at the front of the line. Her steps were slow, stiff and determined, but they, too, counted. Every step forward counted as a victory—for every challenge of her will, and every test of her courage, for sacrifices she thought had been too much to bear, for the ache in her heart. Today wasn't about the choice she would make on a ballot, it was about her right to make it.

Acknowledgments

Each book presents its own set of challenges. Sometimes the challenge is dedicating and balancing writing time with life's other responsibilities, or illness, or grieving the loss of a family member or a friend. Or sometimes a story requires an exceptional amount of research or plot analysis before the writing can even begin. *Tangled Roots* has been no exception to challenge. Since it is set during a time in our history that is different from my own life in so many ways, reading and documentaries proved to be valuable resources for the historical aspects of the story, and my human resources were invaluable to my understanding of the social climate and attitude of the time. For their generous time, whether it was reading drafts or answering questions no matter how insignificant they may have seemed, and for their insights into Southern history, I would like to thank Lynne Pierce, Bett Norris, and Thelma Gordon. Your help was appreciated more than you know.

Of course, the production of any book is the result of the efforts of a team of people, and I am blessed with a remarkable team at Bywater Books. Many thanks are due to the excellent editing skills of Kelly Smith, Jess Wells, and Caroline Curtis, to cover artist Bonnie Liss at Phoenix Graphics, and to the untiring efforts of publisher and publicity director Michele Karlsberg.

Also and always greatly appreciated is the support and encouragement from my friends, family, and partner, who put up with an odd and changeable schedule, and are always there to support my efforts no matter how tired or frustrated I get. For that and more, I thank you.

Bywater Books

UNDER THE WITNESS TREE

Marianne K. Martin

Civil War Secrets inspire a present day love story

An aunt she didn't know existed leaves Dhari Weston with a plantation she knows she doesn't want.

Dhari's life is complicated enough without an antebellum albatross around her neck. Complicated enough without the beautiful Erin Hughes and her passion for historical houses, without Nessie Tinker, whose family breathed the smoke of General Sherman's march and who knows the secrets hidden in the ancient walls—secrets that could pull Dhari into their sway and into Erin's arms.

But Dhari's complicated life already has a girlfriend she wants to commit to, a family who needs her to calm the chaos of her mother's turbulent moods and a job that takes the rest of her time.

The last thing she needs are Civil War secrets that won't lie easy and a woman with secrets of her own . . .

Print ISBN 978-1-932859-00-3
Ebook ISBN 978-1-932859-94-2

Available at your local bookstore
or call 734-662-8815
or order online at www.bywaterbooks.com

Bywater Books

MISS McGHEE

Bett Norris

"Any reader will love this intelligent, richly detailed, altogether satisfying portrayal of a resourceful woman's struggle for love and self-determination in 20th century small-town America. *Miss McGhee* signals the arrival of an impressive, gifted story-teller." —Katherine V. Forrest

World War II is over, and like millions of others, Mary McGhee is looking for a future. A new start, a new job, a new place. But in the small Alabama town she's chosen, she soon finds it's not so easy to leave the past behind.

There's the old problem of being an unwelcome woman in a man's world when Mary takes on the challenge of returning a neglected lumber empire to profitability. Then there's Lila Dubose, the boss's wife, who stirs up desires Mary can't escape, fears she can't control, and reminders that she is surrounded by threat.

Set in the shadow of the civil rights movement, *Miss McGhee* is a sweeping tale of forbidden love in a turbulent time. First-time author Bett Norris portrays one of the darkest and most troubling times in American history with exceptional skill and sensitivity, giving us a unique insight into our own recent history.

Print ISBN 978-1-932859-33-1
Ebook ISBN 978-1-932859-805-1